58% Cabbage

KARL
MacDERMOTT

58% Cabbage

First published in 2021
by Eyewear, an imprint of Black Spring Press Group
Suite 333, 19-21 Crawford Street
Marylebone, London W1H 1PJ
United Kingdom

Cover design and typeset by Edwin Smet
Cover photograph by RichVintage, Getty images
Author photograph by Bernard Walsh

ISBN 978-1-913606-34-3

Printed by TJ Books Limited

For all the gobdaws

CONTENTS

A NEW BEGINNING FOR RODDY BODKIN

'The Modh Coinníollachs were an ancient band of fearsome warriors who roamed the highways and byways of Connacht in the Middle Ages or even sometime before, and who terrorised the local population of pixies, crones and leprechauns. The leader of The Modh Coinníollachs was one of Galway's most infamous sons, a man who made Ivan the Terrible look like Ivan the Perfectly Reasonable – the ruthlessly despotic and legendary High Chief Finbar Proinséas Ó' Ciardhubháin. He was born in 1341. On this exact spot you are standing on now, in front of this fast-food joint called Madra on Quay Street. Madra is the Irish word for dog. Don't worry, the owners do a good line in postmodern irony. And I hear the burgers are very nice. So we'll take a break now from Historical Walking Tours Galway and if any of you want some refreshments you can use one of those vouchers Madra has supplied us with, and I'll see you back here in twenty minutes.'

Roddy Bodkin yawns. Puts down his rucksack.

Takes out a bottle of water. Takes a refreshing gulp. Looks at the six tourists. Three Finns. A Japanese couple. An American. The three Finns smile and go into Madra. The American stands outside with the Japanese couple. There is a pause. The American approaches Roddy.

'These like, Moe Conneelogs, were they like Attila the Hun bad? Like how evil and depraved were these guys?'

Roddy smiles.

'Remember the movie *Braveheart*? They were like those guys. But without the Scottish accents. And the aspirations for self-determination. But with a much stronger capacity for wanton destruction.'

The American nods and walks over to the window of Madra to check the menu. He looks back towards Roddy.

'I love that Mel Gibson.'

Roddy stands to the side and looks at the Japanese couple. He takes out his call and text-only Nokia mobile phone and struggles to read the screen in the bright sun. No missed calls. No texts. No need to put it on mute. Why does he even bother with this yoke? Pointless upgrading to a smartphone. Wouldn't make any difference.

Suddenly he spots his boss. Bartley Higgins. Wearing dark glasses. Under a woolly cap. In a long coat.

Bartley moves closer to Roddy. In a getting-something-off-his-chest manner.

'What's all this shite you're coming up with?'

'I just get a bit bored with the same old stuff. They seem to enjoy it.'

Bartley guides Roddy to the other side of the pedestrianised Quay Street.

'It's complete bollocks, Roddy. Now, we've had complaints before and you were warned a few weeks back. We at Historical Walking Tours Galway have a brand to protect. Newsflash! We are known as Historical Walking Tours Galway. Not Hysterical Walking Tours Galway. If only you *were* hysterical. They're not even funny! Those tall tales you're coming up with.'

'Just trying to liven things up, Bartley. Let's be honest, nothing much has happened in Galway, over the last five hundred years. Even *you* know that.'

'Beside the flippin' point. We're in the business of providing a light-hearted yet fact-based guided tour of the number one city in the West of Ireland, Galway – City of the Tribes, not cock-and-bull stories about marauding bands of bloodthirsty warriors named after the conditional mode of a verb in the Irish language. Do you think you're some sort of a comedian?'

A long pause ensues. Roddy contemplates the matter.

'Yes. Bartley, I think, maybe, I am a comedian. I've always thought I could be good at comedy. Just never got round to trying it.'

'Well then, off you go, Roddy. Hop it. No one is standing in your way. See how you get on making people laugh in the clubs. Go on. Beat it. I'll take over your shift from here. I'll have some major re-telling of historical events to do, but I don't mind. I'm a professional. It's my job.'

'You mean you're letting me go?'

'No. I'm not letting you go. I'm setting you free. I'm giving you an opportunity to fulfil your destiny, make your dreams come true and bring laughter to the world.'

There is a pause.

'Now fuck off!'

AUNTIE EILEEN HAS PASSED AWAY

So, thanks to Bartley Higgins, now is the time to finally bite that comedy bullet. It's never too late. Granted, Roddy is in his early forties. So what? The forties are the new thirties, right? Wizened American comedienne Phyllis Diller started quite late. He read about her on a *Late Bloomers in Comedy* website last week. But who wants to be Phyllis Diller? No. Ricky Gervais. Ricky is the one. Ricky wrote and appeared in *The Office* when he was thirty-eight. Yes. Be like Ricky. Yes. Roddy walks over to a calendar hanging on the wall, in the kitchen of the house he shares with his long-term girlfriend Lorraine. It's the freebie calendar of Martyn Turner's best cartoons from *The Irish Times*. The date is Monday, October 1st, 2012. He makes a solemn pledge. Aloud.

'By Monday, September 30th, 2013 I, Roddy Bodkin, will have launched my stand-up comedy career, be gigging regularly and will have assembled enough material for a one-man show that I plan to take to The Edinburgh Fringe, the following August'.

He takes a biro and writes, over the date in the calendar, 'Comedy Career Deadline'. He stands back. Looks at it. A determined nod follows. He absentmindedly scratches his chin and notices on his thumb some blood from a shaving mishap earlier that morning. Suddenly and dramatically, he smudges his bloodied thumb over the words 'Comedy Career Deadline'. Have to stick to it now, he thinks. Signed off in blood.

'I hereby call this declaration of intent the Comedy Covenant.'

He takes a deep breath, clears his mind of all distractions, picks up his laptop, walks over to the kitchen table, opens the laptop and tries getting down to write some blisteringly funny shit-hot comedy material.

But first...

Can't leave that empty tea cup and dirty spoon lying around. They have to be washed. And dried. And put away. After some more sitting and staring at the blank computer screen, he decides that some TV channels have to be zapped in the next room. A change of screen and scene. May get the creative juices flowing. An old British movie from the 1950s, *Laughter in Paradise,* with one of his favourite actors, Alastair Sim, has just started on

Film4. Only eighty minutes. He'll watch that first. Then, the work will really start! Ten minutes into the movie, the phone rings. He recognises the ring. It doesn't make any sense but he always knows when his mother is calling. The phone rings out and switches to the answering machine. The voice leaves a hesitant message.

'Roddy, this is your mother. Agnes. Eh, your Auntie Eileen is very unwell. So be prepared for the worst. OK, so bye for now. It's Agnes. It's your mother. Agnes. Eh bye. Bye. Agnes.'

Roddy is prepared for the worst. And prepares himself for the worst. By not answering the phone over the next few hours. Because he knows if he does answer the phone and mother tells him Auntie Eileen has passed away, she will want him to go to the removal *and* the funeral. In Waterford. The removal *and* the funeral. We Irish gorge on death. We just can't get enough of it. Where else in the world does a person turn up *twice* to pay one's respects? Twice. See the same faces twice. Go through the same rigmarole twice. Mumble those same lines over and over again.

'Sorry for your loss. She was a lovely woman altogether. Sorry for your trouble.'

Have you mumbled the words to this person?

Have you mumbled the words to that person? Did you mumble the words to this person yesterday or was it that person? Will you mumble the words to this person again, just in case? Roddy is determined to avoid all this mumbling and not be compelled into going to yet another removal and another funeral. This is why he vows not to answer the phone. When Eileen's time is up, his mother will be forced to leave another self-conscious meandering tentative message announcing the death while simultaneously stating who she is four times and Roddy can always claim he listened to the message too late to make the necessary travel arrangements. That is the plan.

But there are times in life when you intend not to do something, and are determined not to do that thing you do not want to do, but a momentary lapse of concentration scuppers all intentions. Or someone else's momentary lapse of concentration. He *had* informed Lorraine. Later, when she got home he'd said, 'Lorraine, if the phone rings, let it ring. It could be mother.' But just after dinner, maybe it was that freshly opened second bottle of red wine after a pre-dinner vodka or two – judgement slightly impaired for both – the minute the phone rings, Lorraine picks it up.

'Hello? Agnes. How are you? I'm grand. Oh. Oh dear. I'm very sorry to hear that. Hang on, he's right here next to me.'

Lorraine mouths a sorry with an appropriately contrite expression as she hands over the phone.

'Hello Roddy, this is your mother.'

'Oh hi.'

'Your Auntie Eileen passed away this morning.'

There is a pause.

'Peacefully.'

In Ireland a person dies 'peacefully', 'suddenly' or 'after a long illness bravely borne'.

Roddy doesn't know what to say.

'Oh well.'

Too blasé? But how should he react? He hasn't seen Auntie Eileen in over twenty years. He has never had an adult conversation with her. Roddy, like a lot of people, reverts back to being an awkward child any time he has had any interaction with his elderly aunts and uncles and if it hadn't been for the fact that Auntie Eileen's vagina was the very first vagina he ever saw, his memory of her would be very vague.

'It's for the best. She wasn't herself the last few years,' mother continues.

The expression the attendant used in the nursing home to describe Auntie Eileen's latter-day mental condition suddenly pops into Roddy's head. His younger brother Ronan had visited her once and told him a nurse had stated Auntie Eileen was 'pleasantly confused'. Auntie Eileen had been in a state of pleasant confusion since 2006.

'Now the removal is at Falconers Funeral Home, Tramore at five o'clock on Monday. The coffin will be moved to St. Catherine's Church by half six and the funeral is Tuesday morning at ten o'clock. Now, obviously Ronan can't go because he's on that business trip to Denmark.'

'Waterford is a bit of a trek.'

'Roddy, I'd go but I'm afraid I'd pick up a bit of a cough on the way, especially at this time of the year with the winter coming in.'

'I don't know. I could have something on.'

'What?'

'Something.'

'The walking tour is it? Can you not ask Bartley to switch with someone?'

Roddy pauses. He hasn't told the world and its mother (or his mother) about his most recent employment hiatus.

'I'll see what I can do.'

'Good man. Your Auntie Eileen has only one

removal.'

'And funeral.'

'I'm asking you to go, Roddy. Special favour for your mother.'

Roddy sighs.

Typical. When he worked all those years at Fleming Travel nobody died. Not one person in his extended family had passed away in that whole period. No one had died tragically or 'before their time'. So he didn't get out of going to any removals or any funerals. But now, they are all dropping like flies. OK, they are all getting older so it makes sense, but couldn't just one of them have died of an unexpected heart attack from the years 1991 to 2004? No. But nowadays it never ends. 2012 has been a bumper year for funerals. He has already gone to five in the last six months. Bartley was surprisingly flexible in that situation. 'Your family are your rock. No problem taking a few days off.' But can he say no to his mother? No. He cannot say no to his mother. No.

'Roddy? Are you still there? You'd be representing the family. You'll have to go. We'll have to have some representation. She was, after all, the sister of your father, the Lord have mercy on him.'

'OK.'

'Don't worry about accommodation. Your cousin Aidan will put you up in his house. They have plenty of room. I've already talked to Fionnuala.'

Roddy puts down the phone. Lorraine looks at him.

'I don't have to go. Do I?'

'No. Don't worry. Our funeral and removal rule still applies. For funerals and removals, if neither of us have met the recently deceased person from our respective families, we don't have to go.'

'But I think I met your Auntie Eileen. Once. At your father's funeral.'

'I see. Luckily you are covered by the stipulation we subsequently added to the rule. If either of us have only met the recently deceased person from our respective families just once, at a prior family wedding or funeral, we are also not obliged to attend their removal or funeral.'

'Goody. Didn't fancy it. And Waterford is such a kip.'

As Roddy sits in that crowded Intercity bus as it slowly navigates its way south-east, his mind is transported back to the summer of 1977. Roddy aged eight. His dad Ger, and his mother Agnes, are taking their first trip away. To Torremolinos. That generation who had grown up during the scarcity of the 1940s and the grimness of the 1950s have finally experienced a small amount of prosperity and have the money and the newfound confidence to holiday in sunnier climes. Roddy, and his only sibling, younger brother Ronan, are left in Ireland. Down in Tramore. With Uncle Roger, Auntie Eileen and their sons Aidan and Maurice.

On his first morning in Tramore, a Saturday morning, Roddy and his two excited cousins wake very early and are making quite a 'racket' playing with Dinky toys on the upstairs landing. Suddenly, Auntie Eileen's bedroom door opens.

In a short kimono-like dressing gown, fashionable at the time, she walks across the landing, berating Aidan and Maurice for breaking the house rules. No playing on the landing. And no noise this hour of the morning. They look on guiltily and start putting the Dinkies away. Roddy, still lost in a mid-*vroom vroom,* looks up abruptly as Auntie Eileen walks towards him, continuing to issue parental edicts to her sons. Suddenly, he recoils in horror. My God, what is *that*? Roddy realises Auntie Eileen isn't wearing any underwear and there is this small woodland animal between her legs.

Roddy remembers being flummoxed for the

rest of his stay. He couldn't get the image out of his head. Was there something wrong with Auntie Eileen? His ten-year-old cousin Yvonne didn't have this affliction. Roddy once saw her... front bottom... as it was referred to, when she dropped a towel at the beach while changing. Not a single solitary hair in that general region. But Auntie Eileen. That was scary. Each time she was nice to him and kissed him goodnight over the following fortnight he'd shudder a little, thinking of that gross furry tuft lodged under her belly button.

Roddy arrives at the funeral home just before five o'clock. He is quite exhausted after what seems like a trek across continents.

He goes up to Aidan.

'Sorry for your loss, Aidan.'

'Thanks for coming,' Aidan says.

He approaches Maurice and decides to vary things.

'Sorry for your trouble, Maurice.'

Maurice nods sadly.

'Sure, what can you do?'

Roddy shrugs in empathy and walks towards the open coffin. Roddy looks at Auntie Eileen for a moment. He has heard the hair of a corpse still grew after death. What about pubic hair? After all these years the image of her bushy member is still quite vivid. Roddy suddenly notices his cousin Jimmy, one of Eileen's other nephews, approach. He nods at Jimmy. Jimmy looks at Auntie Eileen in the open coffin.

'Jeez, she's looking well.'

Roddy stares at his cousin in a slightly baffled manner. He always has difficulty analysing Jimmy. A deadpan master of wit or a complete fool?

Jimmy continues. 'They've done a great job.'

Roddy sighs. Complete fool. No they haven't done a great job Jimmy. Auntie Eileen is definitely *not* looking well. Unless you have an unhealthy fascination with Madame Tussaud's wax figures.

'She went awful fast in the end but at least she didn't linger.'

Actually she did linger, Jimmy. Six years in a pleasantly confused state. That sounds like a lot of lingering, Jimmy.

Jimmy pauses. He becomes slightly tearful, but like all men in Roddy's family, tries to hide his emotion. In doing so, bizarrely, his chin starts to quiver in random involuntary spasms. Jimmy begins to splutter something lowly but can't complete the sentence.

'The poor...'

Roddy becomes alarmed. He knows what Jimmy is attempting to say.

'The poor...'

Roddy exhales tensely.

Jimmy continues. 'The poor... *kray-thur*.' He quickly wipes his eyes and then clears his throat with a contrived cough.

Later. Back in Aidan and Fionnuala's. Having ham sandwiches, coleslaw, currant buns and tea. Bob Dylan once sang 'Time is a jet plane, it moves too fast', but Roddy doesn't find that particular observation apt on this particular occasion. Relatives mingle, tea is refilled, sandwiches are half-finished and memories and old yarns about Auntie Eileen are excavated. The time she was in London during Queen Elizabeth's coronation. The time she'd sprained her ankle climbing the Pyrenees with Roger. The time she'd confronted two burglars in church after mass one Saturday evening. Roddy has heard all these stories before. He is bored, restless. Aidan offers him a glass of whiskey. He takes it gratefully.

The night drags on. Out of politeness people stay. The conversation moves onto different topics. Local political characters and what shenanigans they are up to. The prices of things in various shops. Jimmy, Aidan and Maurice start talking about some under-15s schools soccer team that reached some final. Roddy is offered another whiskey. A generous portion. Sure, that first one was only wetting the glass.

As the talk continues Roddy excuses himself and goes to the bathroom. After he has relieved himself, rather than returning immediately he just sits on the edge of the bath and listens to the voices downstairs. He then flicks through a magazine that has been placed discreetly next to the loo and finds out that wild elephants only need two hours sleep whereas giant armadillos sleep for eighteen hours.

After ten minutes he returns to the living room. His cousins are still debating that under-15s schools soccer final. When he sits down he realises the alcohol is starting to take effect. Roddy isn't a mean drunk but whiskey can be a mean drink.

'Roddy, have you any special memory of Eileen?' another cousin, Joan, inquires.

Roddy smiles. And sighs. He looks down on his whiskey and takes a swig. His slight smirk and strange reaction catches the attention of the others and they quieten down to see what he will say. He has hardly said a word all evening but is respected by his relatives as much as any purposeless work-shy family oddball can be.

'Yeh. Roddy. You must have one or two memories. When you stayed here with Ronan in 1977 for example,' Aidan contributes. 'Something we haven't heard yet.'

Roddy nods in recognition.

'Ah. 1977. Something you haven't heard yet.'

In the midst of some forty-two-percent-proof fuzzy thinking, he starts to make a few frenzied calculations. Is this an opportunity too good to pass? There will be repercussions. One side of the family will never speak to him again. But is that necessarily a bad thing? No more of these cloyingly oppressive evenings. Agnes will never forgive him but on the upside she will never ask him to go to a family funeral again.

'Come on Roddy, any special memories of Eileen?' Joan persists.

He giggles. He downs the remainder of his latest glass of whiskey. What the hell. Time to throw caution to the wind. And do some carping of the diem.

'I have one memory. One striking memory.'

The interest in the room is building.

'You could almost say it was indelible...'

'Go on, Roddy. What is it?'

'Yes Roddy, you have to tell us now.'

'OK'.

Roddy sighs and leans back.

'Just something that for some odd reason left a mark.'

'Tell us, Roddy.'

Roddy fiddles with the empty whiskey glass and then stares across the room. He speaks slowly.

'Auntie Eileen's vagina...'

There is a pause. More like a mute interlude. A very lengthy mute interlude.

'Auntie Eileen's vagina was the first vagina I ever saw.'

In all his forty-three years Roddy Bodkin has never experienced such a silence. In a perverse way he relishes the silence. He looks around at the stunned faces. This will be his last family funeral. Mission accomplished.

Cousin Jimmy attempts to break the silence. At first, he starts to mumble lowly.

'Well, funny you should say that.'

Jimmy is greeted with communal bewilderment.

'Actually, it happened to me too. When I was staying here in the summer of 1978.'

He continues, gathering confidence.

'There was something about Auntie Eileen and her lack of underwear during those ten days in August.'

Joan looks sheepish. But why should she, she wonders? Now that the secret is out.

'I was playing with my doll, while staying here, in the summer of 1979, under the kitchen table, and I looked up and I saw her... it... as well... so uh, it was a bit of a shock, like, and I did wonder about it for many years.'

Distant second cousins, Terence and Niall, completely anonymous up to now, decide to contribute.

'We were only here that one time, in May 1981, but yes, it was the case that we too, happened to see Eileen's...'

Roddy leans back in complete astonishment. Mixed with a nagging disappointment. This isn't going exactly to plan. All the cousins making their own disclosures and declarations! He feels a bit like Kirk Douglas. The whole episode is turning into that 'I am Spartacus' moment, if you replace the words 'am Spartacus' with the words 'saw Auntie Eileen's vagina.'

Aidan interrupts.

'Look it, she wasn't an exhibitionist or anything. Swanning around like some pampered film star on the Riviera. I think Mammy was prone to urinary tract infections especially during the summer so she used to walk around with no underwear much of the time because that area has to breathe like.'

Cousin Luke, the doctor in the family, reluctantly gets involved.

'Actually, I'm sorry to intercede because I know it is a delicate matter, but being involved in the medical profession, I'd be familiar with this issue and the last thing you do if you have a UTI is to walk around the place with no underwear.'

Maurice nods.

'OK. Right. Thanks for that, Luke.'

There is another long pause.

'Was she some sort of a naturist, maybe?' next-door neighbour Rory Duffy muses aloud. 'And there's nothing wrong with being a naturist. Maybe she was a sort of a semi-clothed domestic naturist?'

Maurice finally speaks.

'No Rory, she wasn't. Look it, I think we've discussed mammy's vagina enough.'

Aidan sighs. Looks on blankly.

‘Seems like those currant buns haven’t been touched. Would anyone like one?’

RODDY AND LORRAINE

Roddy first notices the smoke while his girlfriend Lorraine is caressing his perineum with that light blue ostrich feather. Lorraine had insisted on lighting a scented candle to enhance the romantic atmosphere. Roddy always wondered why women love candles. Candles cause fires. Fires cause death. Lorraine looks at him.

'What's wrong? You usually enjoy the feather on the perineum.'

'The curtains are on fire.'

The damage to their house on Whitestrand Avenue is substantial. They decide to temporarily move in with Lorraine's parents, Tom and Eucharia, just outside Galway City, in Mervue. Tom looks like a short tubby cardinal in a jumper and Eucharia is a big fan of leggings, angora cardigans and has the most amazing beehive hairstyle. Forty years out of date. A legacy of her time performing with Moate's caucasian version of The Supremes, the Irish girl group singing sensation from 1965 – Maisie and The Missalettes.

Roddy is not completely comfortable with the

arrangement. Tom and Eucharia are very welcoming. But their bull mastiff, Chappy?

'He'll get used to you, Roddy. Don't worry,' Eucharia tells him the first night as she restrains the psychotically aggressive Chappy.

'He's really very cuddly.'

Later that night Roddy awakes. He needs to pee. Gets out of bed, and quietly opens the guest bedroom door. He is greeted by a very low, ominous, persistent growl. Bladder-emptying is deferred. He returns to bed.

'I can't stay here with that dog. In all these years I've visited, he's always had it in for me.'

Lorraine, half-awake, adjusts some duvet.

'He's really very cuddly.'

He isn't very cuddly. He is frightening. And dangerous. And he hates Roddy. All dogs hate Roddy. Tails of friendly dogs stop manically wagging on the immediate sight of him. Inoffensive placid mutts transform themselves into crazed barking sentries when he passes garden gates. Ancient dogs, grey around the mouth and too decrepit to move, raise themselves from their slumber and find a heretofore untapped supply of energy and snarl threateningly at him, temporarily re-living former days of growling glory. Puppies – yes, puppies – start their first fight with him. Roddy knows the situation with himself and Chappy will only end in tears. His.

So quick thinking is called for.

Sadly lacking in the quick thinking department, Roddy eventually decides to ring his friend, forthright farmer, scribbler poet and dog owner Ambrose Hegarty for advice but before he can make the call, at the following morning's breakfast, Eucharia beams at both himself and Lorraine.

'A few months ago, Tom won a holiday for two in a raffle at the Oughterard Golf Club. To New Orleans. I mentioned it way back. Now, we were meant to fly out next weekend for a week but we were talking this over last night and we thought while your house is being rewired and fixed up, why don't the two of you take the holiday instead and go off to the Big Easy? I hear they've done a great job altogether in reconstructing the place after Hurricane Katrina a few years back.'

Overjoyed, Lorraine gets up and hugs Eucharia.

'Are you sure, mum?'

'No problem. It'll be nice for the two of you to get away. Think of it as a sort of Halloween break.'

'I think I need a break, mum. Have been swamped at work lately. Gráinne can pick up some of the slack for a while.'

Lorraine then looks at Roddy. He isn't as enthusiastic. Despite being involved in various aspects of the tourist industry for much of his working life, Roddy is not a great traveller and himself and Lorraine had spent their last holiday in Tuam. Roddy always wonders why people go to so much trouble traipsing off to some far off place only to have to turn round again and come back to where they were. He also doesn't like things 'to be sprung on him.' He needs time to process sudden propositions. A lot of time. And all this is *very* sudden. Lorraine's smile vanishes. Expecting to be disappointed, she is about to decline the offer when Tom enters the kitchen with a, on entrance boisterous, but now having spotted Roddy, dementedly combative and jaw-grinding Chappy.

Looking at his frothing canine nemesis, Roddy has a decision to make. He stares over at Lorraine. And then scrutinises and listens to Chappy. He leans forward on the table and addresses Eucharia.

'Being a huge fan of Dixieland Jazz, and a student of authentic early-to-mid-twentieth-century Americana, I would dearly love to go to New Orleans. Thank you both so much.'

So Roddy and Lorraine end up flying long-haul

from Shannon Airport to New Orleans. Looking down with horror from thirty-three thousand feet, Roddy comforts himself with the knowledge that if the plane crashes not only will he be killed but so too will Simon Cowell who he's spotted in first class while boarding. Every time they hit turbulence on the journey he grabs Lorraine's hand.

'At least that Svengali of musical dross Simon Cowell will die too.'

'What do you mean?'

'He's on the plane.'

Roddy points to where Simon Cowell is sitting.

Mid-flight, when the weather has settled, Lorraine goes to the loo. A few minutes later she retakes her seat.

'That's not Simon Cowell.'

Suddenly the plane starts to gyrate forcefully. More turbulence. Roddy grabs hold of her hand again.

'Are you sure? You mean, we'll die in vain?'

He has calmed down once they finally touch down in Louis Armstrong New Orleans International Airport although he is still slightly worried that their prospective taxi driver might make a detour on the taxi ride to the hotel, introduce them to his friend Monsieur Machete, dice them up and use them as added ingredients to his jambalaya but in his calmer moments Roddy realises this trip is an opportunity to get away from Galway for a week and recharge his relationship with his tolerant girlfriend and maybe he'll come up with some ideas for that blisteringly funny shit-hot comedy material he is meant to be working on. The clock is ticking on that one year deadline. A month has nearly passed on the Comedy Covenant. It is already late October.

What's with this comedy obsession? Lorraine has been asking him for years. Dunno. He's just always loved comedy. Even as a child. When asked in primary school what he wanted to be when he grew up, Roddy answered a comedian or a priest. In retrospect, not a bad answer. Both occupations have much in common. Both comedians and priests get up on a stage. Do their act. Usually a lot of stuff people have heard before. And if they are any good, by the end of the gig, the crowd is eating out of their hands. In a comedian's case, figuratively. In a priest's case, literally.

Roddy's interest in comedy was further sparked by Mr. Maguire's debating society in secondary school. Roddy relished participating in those debates. Passing a witty comment while making a point. Earning the approval and appreciation of the class. Then, sometime later, during his first year at University College Galway (B.A. Hons in English and Geography... *in his fuckin' dreams*... dropped out after failing his repeated repeats) he emceed a few charity gigs and music nights in the Smokey Joe's canteen on campus. He relished getting up on stage, entertaining those scruffy pimply freshmen like himself. All that warmth, energy and attention directed towards him as he introduced the next act. 'What a great feeling,' he thought, 'this is what I want to do'.

But, by second year in college, when he was still repeating first year, gloom descended. He wondered, can people who repeat first year still be referred to as freshmen? Maybe they should be called... stalemen? The lustre of college life had dimmed. His grades remained pitiful. And to (French) cap it off there was that awkward fumbling love affair with a Siouxsie without The Banshees look-alike called Dympna. After two years it was time to accept ignominy and exit academia forever. Completely out of character, for a while he considered heading to Nepal to try and find himself. But father Ger exploded 'Find yourself? You wouldn't even find Nepal! Mr. He-who-studied-Geography-for-two-years-and-couldn't-pass-a-feckin'-exam! No more talk about Nepal now, you'll get up off your arse and take that job I've organised for you!'

Ah yes. The travel agency. The beginning of thirteen long years working for Mr. Fleming, an old friend of Ger's, at Fleming Travel on Mary Street. Then the double whammy of the internet and 9/11 creating a perfect storm and like weather-worn seafront deck chairs being cleared away at the onset of autumn, travel agents were no more.

Since then, he's drifted. Somewhat. Moving from one low-paid job to another low-paid job. Long before anyone else was doing it. Almost a trailblazer and true pioneer in the whole gig economy universe. He was an internet provider sales rep. Another internet provider's customer care service rep. Bicycle courier. Security guard at a circus. Guy who holds sign for shop closing down sale. Guy holding smaller sign for shop closing down sale standing next to guy holding a larger sign publicising the arrival of a new international clothes chain. And then back to the world of tourism with the three and a half years at Historical Walking Tours Galway.

But all that's in the past. And now it's time for

some serious pivoting. And new beginnings in the comedy sphere.

However, as the week away in New Orleans gathers momentum, moments of joke-writing inspiration become as infrequent as Satchmo singing falsetto. By the first two days they have sampled a po' boy and some palate-scorching creole gumbo and have taken an obligatory Louisiana Swamp Tour (never again – not one alligator came to the surface or made an appearance in over three hours!) but Roddy, ever the reluctant traveller, is still quite nervy. Intimidated by all he has read about crime in the Big Easy and that recent serial killing spree near Lafayette, he insists that each afternoon by five o'clock they will be on that St. Charles Streetcar heading back to their hotel. After four evenings in the hotel room Lorraine, however, is becoming restless. Also the couple next door are extremely loud in the grunting and moaning coital ecstasy department. And what stamina! Jesus, Mary, Joseph and the donkey, do those two have stamina!

On the fifth night Lorraine, tiring of all the inactivity, wants to go to a jazz concert but Roddy stands firm. It will just be a bunch of white guys with pot bellies wearing bowler hats. It won't be Johnny Dodds. It won't be Jelly Roll Morton. It won't be Louis Armstrong. It won't be authentic-early-to-mid-twentieth-century Americana. Lorraine is not impressed.

'So, we're not going out to a gig because Louis Armstrong is dead?'

'No. We're not going to a gig because it's not Louis Armstrong and it's not 1928.'

'So, if Louis Armstrong was still alive you still wouldn't go?'

'Yes. It would have to be young Louis Armstrong. Seminal Louis Armstrong. Vital Louis Armstrong. 1928 Louis Armstrong.'

'That's rubbish. Because if you were alive in 1928 and Louis Armstrong was playing down the road, you being you, you still wouldn't go. You'd be saying who is that guy with the trumpet creating that cacophony? You'd want to sit at home and listen to your Debussy records. No, you wouldn't even own one of those wind-up phonograph player things because you wouldn't trust modern technology, so you'd just sit at home and... spit into a spittoon or whatever they did back in 1928.'

Lorraine has a point. Roddy never appreciates anything new.

'A valid observation, darling. I hated reggae in the 1980s but now am quite partial to some Toots and the Maytals.'

'They're playing in Baton Rouge tomorrow night. I saw a flyer advertising it downstairs in the lobby. Want to go?'

Lorraine's suggestion has come out of nowhere. But that is Lorraine Heuston. Always coming up with plans. Suggesting 'things to do.' And if one thing doesn't work out there are always alternatives. Lorraine Heuston's head consists of a whole list of Plan B's and alternative strategies. This momentarily throws Roddy. He needs to get his bearings and gather his thoughts.

'It's not the original Toots. It's like their nephews. Or distant cousins. Or grandchildren. Or just some Jamaican guys.'

'If it was the originals, would you go?'

'No. I'm not *that* partial to them. Let's just stay in. It's a dangerous town out there. They say it's the second murder capital of America. After Washington D.C.'

Lorraine sighs.

'You know the trouble with you, Roddy Bodkin? You are scared of life. Remember that quote you told me years ago? That guy, what was his name? Russell. Bertrand Russell. Yeh. That's his name. He once said that if you live in fear you are already three-quarters dead.'

'Well, at least you are one quarter alive! One always has to look for the positives. Let's stay in and watch *The Mentalist* on TV!'

'We can do that in Galway! Anyway there's ads every three minutes! You can't watch anything on the telly over here with all the ad breaks.'

She pauses and stares at him.

'Roddy, this is a surprise mid-winter break for a few days. Let's make the most of it. *I'm* going to make the most of it. I'm going out!'

'What do you mean, you're going out? Where?'

'I don't know. Out.'

She grabs her bag, turns and shuts the hotel room door on her way out. Roddy remains seated. Will he really let her go out on her own, all alone, in New Orleans? Or, conversely, does he want to be stuck, for the rest of the night, alone, in a hotel room in New Orleans? Almost on cue the grunting and moaning starts up next door. Jesus, Mary, Joseph and the donkey where do those two get their... bonking indefatigability?

As the sound level starts to increase, he decides, after all, to follow Lorraine.

They end up going to a jazz club off North Rampart Street in the French Quarter and watch

Syd Palmer and His Syncopated Sidemen. As Syd, in a bowler hat, and those seven other fat white guys in pot bellies start warbling 'When The Saints Go Marching In', Roddy wonders what would cause him the more excruciating discomfort in life, listening to this or sharing kennel space with the dog called Chappy?

THE COMEDY WORKSHOP

'The thing with somebody heckling you is you can't ignore it but you shouldn't burst out crying either. I used to cry a lot in the very early days when I was heckled. I don't know. I guess I'm just a sensitive person. As time went on, I learned to compose myself more on stage but to be honest I was never great with hecklers heckling my act. As a comedian there is that three-second time frame that needs to be adhered to stringently when responding to a heckle, but sometimes sadly I fell outside that time frame. On occasions, it was minutes. Once, during a gig in Letterkenny, I think I clocked up an hour and three-quarters; everyone had gone home, staff were cleaning the glasses and I was still on stage pondering a witty comeback.'

Roddy is admiring comedian Cormac Creedon's honesty. He spotted the upcoming Comedy Workshop poster just inside the door of Charlie Byrne's bookshop the previous week. Nun's Island Arts Centre. Wednesday the 12th. 11pm to 4pm. Fifty euro. Facilitator Cormac Creedon. Bit steep, he thought. But he really did have to start putting some sort of structure to those comedy dreams.

But Roddy's natural propensity for negativity started kicking in almost immediately. What could he learn from this comedy has-been? A has-been? Not even a has-been. A permanent never was! Like a lot of people who are not completely successful in their chosen creative area, veteran comedian Cormac Creedon had branched out into the 'mentoring' arena over the last few years. A frank admission of moribund career and complete irrelevance. Cormac had achieved a speck of notoriety in the 1980s as Ireland's only home-based anti-Irish comedian. Spent a lot of time in hospital in that period also after being regularly assaulted after gigs but he'd largely recovered by now apart from some ongoing mobility issues. Roddy remembered seeing Cormac on *The Late Late Show* in the early 1990s. The audience didn't really 'get it'. Roddy didn't really 'get it' either but recalled one joke that received a puzzled groan – 'The Irish are fierce thick, aren't they? I met this fella in a pub in Thurles once, thought The Gaza Strip was Paul Gascoigne with no clothes on.'

But forthright farmer scribbler poet Ambrose Hegarty, best friend of Roddy Bodkin, persuaded Roddy to go to the workshop. He'd go along too if Roddy wanted some moral support.

'Roddy, I'm a big fan of the comedy as well, like. Anyway, I've written some hard-edged comic verse over the years. Sort of like John Cooper Clarke meets uh... Pam Ayres. Wouldn't mind trying to rework it a bit. Also, I want to ask Cormac about my theory.'

'What theory, Ambrose?'

'The one about the sinister correlation between the growth in the number of coffee shops and the growth in the number of comedians in Ireland. Before 1995 there were hardly any coffee shops or comedians in this country. But suddenly within the last two decades, or so, both sectors have proliferated like the Gremlins having fertility treatment. I wonder, will Cormac agree that there could be a connection? Even some kind of conspiracy? Think about it. The government wants the public to laugh more. When they're laughing they're not thinking about all that is going wrong with the country. So I believe what happens is, the government is in cahoots with the coffee manufacturers and coffee shops, something is put in the coffee, making more of us turn into comedians. More comedians, more comedy clubs. More comedy clubs, more laughter. More laughter, more distraction and people stop thinking about the day-to-day problems in our society. Call me a far-fetched borderline unhinged conspiracy theorist Roddy, but I smell something fishy and it's not just coffee beans!'

'I think you're online too much and are developing a paranoid mindset.'

'Look it, Roddy, I just want to ask him the question. Does he think the exponential increase of caffeine intake in countless coffee shops over the last two decades has fuelled the thousandfold increase of nascent local mirth-makers – who aren't that fuckin' funny, I might add!'

'I agree with that, wholeheartedly.'

'Just too many of them. Monaghan poet and misanthrope Paddy Kavanagh said in the 1950s that you could have a standing army of 100,000 poets in Ireland. Nowadays, it's a standing army of 100,000 stand-up comedians.'

'Sadly.'

'You know the fuckers I really hate, Roddy. The ones I call ballpark impressionists. There's too many of them in this country. The sort of impressionists who do ballpark impersonations of various local politicians and sports personalities. The impersonation is sort of like the guy they're trying to do but it's not really like the guy. Fuck off ballpark impressionist, that's not Willie O'Dea, that's you with a moustache standing in a hole in the ground! Fuck off ballpark impressionist that's not Mary O'Rourke, that's you in a bad wig doing an over-the-top lisp. Fuck off ballpark impressionist that's not Roy Keane, that's you just looking a bit deranged while doing a generic Cork accent! Do you get what I'm talking about?'

'Yeh.'

'Time to conclude rant?'

'Yeh.'

So, a hundred euro the poorer, on the day of the comedy workshop, Roddy and Ambrose sit in a modestly attended space, as Cormac Creedon covers many areas in navigating a working life in comedy. He offers some career advice.

'When you are starting off, take every gig offered. I was doing this gig once and I was getting no laughs. Nothing. It was awful. Like playing a day room in a hospice. Actually it *was* a day room in a hospice. It was my agent Sisyphus' idea, the near legendary – for all the wrong reasons – Sisyphus O'Shea of SOS Management. He'd say 'No matter where, you have to get up there and perform. You must learn your craft.' I said to him, 'But Sisyphus, a hospice?' He'd say 'Sure what are you moaning about? They're not dead yet. They're still breathing. Anyway, think of the upside, they probably won't heckle you. They've got bigger things on their mind than your act, more important issues to mull over like fatal diseases and encroaching mortality or whatever. What I'm saying is this, they'll be a placid crowd, probably sedated out of their minds, but they'll be lovely. Trust me.' And he was right. I felt better after doing that gig. I mean, I was dying up there and they were dying down there but it was all part of the experience.'

Cormac expands on the topic of representation.

'Picking the correct agent is a very important step in the career of any up-and-coming stand-up comedian. Now, if I had to do it again I would never have gone with Sisyphus. First thing he said to me after he caught my act was 'I don't think you're funny ha-ha. You're not funny peculiar. You're more funny unfunny. But I'll take you on because I hear there's a lot of money to be made in this auld comedy lark.' So, for somebody who should have been supporting me artistically, he was never truly behind me. An agent should be a friend. A cajoler. A social worker. Sisyphus was none of these. And on a sheer practical level he was useless as an agent. You see Sisyphus had a phobia about using telephones, some hygiene thing, and for an agent that's just disastrous, and that fax machine could hardly fit into his camper van/office. When I saw him training those homing pigeons, I knew it was time for us to part ways.'

Cormac also has some perceptive things to say on performance.

'Your first thirty seconds are essential. Once you walk out on that stage, the audience has to know who you are, what you're about. You have to establish that very quickly and build that bridge to the audience. That's why your first gag is so important. In a way it has to sum you up in essence. It helps enormously if they like you from the word go. It's so important. They have to know who you are and immediately know where you are coming from. Then they'll go along with you and what you have to say. I sort of lost my way after I stopped being Ireland's only home-based anti-Irish comedian. To be honest, I'd never gotten huge laughs with the act. But I'd always received a few genuine smiles and sympathetic titters from the crowd. But suddenly – there was nothing! One old song from the 1960s sums the audience reaction during that period of my comedy career. Simon and Garfunkel's 'The Sound of Silence'. I felt

I needed to change my image. Decided my material should become darker. More confrontational. Edgy. Tried a Dennis Leary or Bill Hicks approach. Started wearing a black eye patch. Just to be different, you know. Create a look. The comedian with the black eye patch. Trouble is, it affected my sight line and I fell off a stage once in Clonakilty. Broke my collar-bone.'

Given his own problems with writing material, Roddy asks a question.

'Material. How difficult is it to produce stuff, Cormac?'

'Very tough. I myself did go through a difficult period trying to come up with new material and there were rumours on the circuit that I used to steal other comedians' jokes. Not true. Technically. I wouldn't call it stealing. I saw myself more, in that time, as a covers comedian. I was covering other comedians' material. Like a covers band. In fact, in a way I was paying tribute to their material by covering it. But I was completely blackballed and ostracised by the other comedians. It was a real low point in my career.'

A young attractive woman called Claire raises her hand.

'What are the chances of making it big?'

Cormac sighs.

'Well, we all start off wanting to make it big. But you become more realistic the older you get. When I was young, I wanted to be Woody Allen. Now I'd be happy being Foster & Allen.'

The participants laugh.

'In a nutshell, that sums up the trajectory of one's dreams. From striving to be a world-famous ground-breaking New York comedy genius with a slightly complicated and deeply unsavoury interaction with close family members to settling for being a completely mediocre, frankly irritating, always working, accordion-driven midlands musical duo.'

There is a pause. Cormac continues.

'But everyone wants to know about the chances of success. When we look back on our lives all of us hope to reflect fondly on a reservoir of success. Not a slurry pit of failure.'

There is a loud guffaw from the back of the room. A worryingly thin birdlike woman hidden in an oversized muslin scarf finds the term 'slurry pit of failure' uproariously funny.

Cormac continues.

'However, unfortunately, in show business, and I hate having to be brutally honest, most of us end up in that slurry pit.'

Cormac notices the alarm on the faces of some of the participants. He needs to lighten things up.

'But that doesn't mean success is impossible. The soul singer James Brown once said the secret to show business success is teeth and hair. So find a great dentist and buy a good conditioner and away we go!'

There is a muted chuckle. The mood has turned more positive again. Cormac leans back on a table, arms folded, and feels the time is right for his big set piece theory. One he has recounted many times in comedy workshops and one he is still very impressed with.

'Success in comedy is like a chair. An IKEA chair that you have to construct from the catalogue. The seat of the chair and the four legs to the chair. Firstly, the seat of the chair. That's you. But if the seat of the chair doesn't have a secure foundation and isn't rooted in something authentic and likeable it's going to collapse and you'll end up on your arse.'

Laughter consumes the room.

'But not only does the seat have to be secure, with whatever they supply in those little nuts and bolts bags, the four legs of the chair have to be solid and also positioned in the correct order. The four legs of the chair that ensure success are, 1. Talent. You have to have a bit of talent. First leg of the chair. 2. Hard work. You need to work so hard, no messing around. Second leg of the chair. 3. Luck. You need that bit of luck. The right time in the right place. The third leg of the chair. 4. Force of personality. Strength of character. You need to be a strong-willed, fully focused individual. Ruthless, even. Now, we have the fourth leg of the chair. And with the seat and the four legs of the chair properly constructed the chair is now a success!'

'Were you a sturdily constructed chair, Cormac?' Claire asks.

Cormac sighs.

'More like a stool.'

The self-deprecation gets another big laugh from the attendees.

'A two-legged stool. In hindsight, I wasn't the full package. Like when some of the bits are missing, when you open the IKEA box. And there's not much to do, if you don't make it. Irish comedians have it tough. If an American comedian doesn't make it in America, he can always go to England because the English are infatuated with all things American. And the English comedian, if he doesn't make it in England, he can always come over here to Ireland, because we are very impressed with English comedians. Because they are from London and they *must be good*. But if an Irish comedian doesn't make it in Ireland, where does he go? Actually, he goes to The Isle of Man. You would be amazed by the amount of failed Irish comedians making a living in the Isle of Man. In fact, that's where I'm living presently. In Douglas.'

There is a pause in proceedings. The workshop participants become reflective. Where will their show business dreams ultimately lead them? To the dead end cul-de-sac of disappointment? Will they be forever strolling those boulevards of oblivion? Gold card members of the What-Might-Have-Been Club?

Cormac notices the sudden lull. He has a suggestion.

'Well, I think it's time for a small coffee break. There's a new coffee shop a few doors down. See you all back here in twenty minutes?'

A hand shoots up from the back of the room. Ambrose clears his throat.

'Actually before we break Cormac, can I seek your opinion and that of the room, on, funnily enough, a coffee shop related matter?'

A PROPOSAL OF MARRIAGE 1963

Ger Bodkin was born in 1932 in Athenry, a village twelve miles outside Galway City. Like many of his generation he was quite musical and loved to play the piano in his family home, but growing up he was constrained by the stultifying world that was the Ireland of the late 1930s and early 1940s. As a young man he read many books – the ones the authorities allowed its citizens to read – loved Hopalong Cassidy movies and was a closet cricket fan. By 1952 he had got his first job, in Powell's Music Shop on William Street, and though, in the back of his mind, he still longed to be the Eddy Duchin of Galway, he was grateful to have a job. Any job.

Despite his quasi-musical leanings and vague artistic aspirations, Ger, in his early pre-contrarian days, was essentially a conformist, a daily communicant who wore his pioneer's pin with pride. And one balmy evening in September 1959, at the Seapoint dance hall, in the still undeveloped seaside resort of Salthill, he first set eyes on Agnes Fennelly.

Agnes Fennelly wore glasses. A short woman

with a no-nonsense steely determination and a proactive stride she had inherited from her father, Cornelius Fennelly. A diligent farm girl who had completed a secretarial course and had just started work in a solicitor's office on Eyre Street, she had noticed the tall, balding Ger a few weeks previously, parking his bicycle before entering the dance hall. And now he had noticed her.

For a few months after that, nothing much happened. Courtship was slow in those days. Very slow. The dances were quite formal and consisted of dance band music with a travelling orchestra recreating the hits of the day. As 'I'll Be With You in Apple Blossom Time' wafted in the background, soft drinks, tea and sandwiches would be served but there was strictly no alcohol. Inhibitions weren't loosened but put on the back burner by innocent inter-gender flirting and innuendo-free banter. People seemed to enjoy themselves but there was no overstepping the line. No hanky-panky. No misbehaving. It was a mating ritual without any mating.

One night the following November, Ger, leaving the dance, went over to his parked bicycle but noticed he had a puncture. Agnes, with her new friend Rita, was also coming out of the dance hall.

They had recently started sharing digs on Newcastle Road under the watchful eye of an old widow, Mrs. Moynihan. Their bicycles were parked next to Ger's. Showing some of that steely determination, Agnes Fennelly seized her moment.

'Have you got a flat tyre?'

Ger scratched his head. Wasn't used to talking to women.

'Have. Sure, I'll be home in two hours if I start walking.'

'We have two bikes here. Me and Rita can go on hers. You can take my one if you want. As long as you return it.'

Agnes laughed a little. Rita, looking at Agnes, was taken aback by her forwardness. Ger was lost for words and though grateful for Agnes's offer and an opportunity to see her again, immediately and instinctively shut out that possibility.

'Ah no. I don't want you to be putting yourself out. Sure, I could be some corner boy for all ye know. No. I'll walk. Thanks, anyway.'

Agnes sighed. Rita nodded. Ger looked down on his puncture. Then fate intervened. Not for the first time in its five-hundred-year history, it started to rain heavily on the city of Galway. Agnes grabbed the handlebars of her bicycle and directed them at Ger.

'Come on. You'll get soaked.'

Ger cycled home with them and bade them farewell on a wet Newcastle Road. He made a mental note of the address. Thirty-three. The age Jesus died. And promised to return the bike the following day.

Thus started a long tortuous three-year courtship. In those days you were a fast woman if you went the whole way. Agnes wasn't a fast woman and didn't go any of the way. Ger didn't seem to mind and, ever the gentleman, waited patiently. No one else was going the whole way – or if they were they weren't talking about it – so he didn't feel he was missing out on anything. It was the norm not to go the whole, if not any, of the way. These were the times they lived in. Anyway, it was against the Lord's teachings. And if they did succumb to temptation – not that they would because Agnes never went any of the way – Agnes could be impregnated and that would be a fate worse than death. Or marrying a Protestant.

Sure, Ger was a red-blooded male and had urges, but when he did, he just went to confession and masturbated in the confession box. Yes. This was Ger Bodkin's dark secret of shame. It was all that talk about sex. In that confession box. All those impure thoughts and impure deeds that Fr. McNamara kept harping on about. One day the previous March, Ger suddenly became aroused listening to Fr. McNamara tell him all the things he was not allowed to think about, or, God forbid, do, and after developing a blackboard duster sized erection that first time, he could not restrain himself on subsequent occasions. Thereafter, a trip to confession was something to enjoy. Only on the days Fr. McNamara was on duty, however. There was just something in the way that flat pious Mayo accent described various banned sexual acts that caused Ger to have the most exquisite self-administered orgasms. Whereas with Fr. Roche's comical Cavan accent there was no way Ger could be stimulated. And the less said about Fr. Helly's whiny interminable Cork brogue the better.

Ger was in a bind. Constant guilt about masturbating caused him to go to confession which caused him to masturbate. Which caused him to feel guilty. Which caused him to go to confession. Which caused him to masturbate. It had to stop.

He'd have to get married.

He decided to pop the question in April 1963. After a Friday evening date. Dates in those days consisted of holding hands and going to the 'flicks'. Ger and Agnes went two or three nights a week to the cinema. Galway back then had many cinemas including The Estoria near Nile Lodge, The Savoy on Eglington Street and The Town Hall Cinema next to the River Corrib and Galwegians of all walks of life watched Robert Mitchum, Kim Novak, Rock Hudson, Deborah Kerr, Gregory Peck and Grace Kelly and a whole array of more obscure stars like Jeff Chandler, Susan Hayward, Wendell Corey, Dorothy Malone, Gig Young and Arlene Dahl. Glamorous technicolour people in faraway places doing glamorous technicolour things. And in that distant Hollywood dream world the sun was always shining. And the ladies wore white gloves and the men had Brylcreem in their hair, wore light-coloured suits, and drove enormous gleaming Cadillacs. They had money. They had optimism. They had elevators.

As Ger sat next to Agnes watching Henry Fonda in Alfred Hitchcock's *The Wrong Man* – though made in 1957 it had taken six years to screen in Galway, another example of things being slower in those days – he worked on a formulation of words to help him pop the question later in Lydon's Restaurant on Shop Street.

Ger knew what he had in the self-abuse department he lacked in the eloquent, romantic, sweet-nothings-in-your-ear department. What do you say to a woman whom you want to marry? As they waited for their tea and cakes on the soft plush burgundy seats of Lydon's Restaurant, Ger inhaled and stared at Agnes solemnly.

'Would you like to be buried with my people?' he suddenly blurted out.

It was the only marriage proposal he could think of. One used frequently in his parents' time. In a strangely ironic way it sort of got straight to the point about marriage. Once you agree, it is a kind of death. Sadly for Ger, Agnes was lost in her own thoughts and was not aware that this question was linked, in any way, whatsoever, to a request for her hand in matrimony.

'What do you mean?'

'When you die?'

Agnes looked extremely puzzled. She probed for clarity.

'Like if I was visiting your family, and we were having a cup of tea but there was a nuclear war with the Russians and there was a massive explosion over Galway or something, is it?'

'Nuclear war? No. That's not what I'm on

about.'

'Or maybe like we were all on a mountaineering trip, me, you, and your family and suddenly there was a colossal avalanche and we lost our footing...'

'No. No Agnes. My people wouldn't be climbers. They've never liked heights. They come from flat country. In fact, mammy has suffered from dreadful vertigo over the years.'

'Well, what do you mean, then?'

'What I mean like is... When you die, would you like to be put into the ground in my family plot.'

'Why?'

'Well, because I'll be there, that's if I die before you, obviously if I haven't died and you die before me I won't be there yet, but statistically men usually die before women... Anyway eventually, mark my words, I will be there and you'll be there and we'll all be there and...'

'What's wrong with you? Why all this talk about burial and death. That's all a bit morbid.'

Ger clammed up. This wasn't going as planned. What would he do now? Seemed like more visits to confession. Indefinitely. But Fr. McNamara was still on that trip to Lourdes and wouldn't be back for a fortnight. And it didn't work with Helly and Roche. There was that new priest, Fr. O' Driscoll from Sligo, near enough to Mayo, might give him a go at the weekend. Agnes, after fiddling for a moment with the zip of her new handbag, looked over at Ger and spoke.

'Listen I was thinking. Do you want to get married?'

HEUSTON, WE HAVE A PROBLEM

'I'm Lorraine Heuston. As CEO and member of the leadership team of Zeitgeist Technologies, I work with the team to create and refine, on an ongoing basis, the strategy of the company based on our purpose and vision.'

Roddy sips his coffee and continues watching his girlfriend's recently uploaded corporate video.

'In my role, I must ensure that the leadership team has the resources and support it needs to successfully execute and operationalise our strategy. As with any successful organisation, it is mostly about letting people do their job and ensuring they are empowered at all levels to do so.'

Roddy dunks a biscuit into his coffee and wonders where do people learn to speak like that? Is there a special diploma in mastering business-speak gibberish? Lorraine, sitting in her office, looks remarkably self-assured onscreen. She proceeds confidently over the clichéd corporate video synth and drum backbeat.

'To a large degree, my part revolves around our external stakeholder relationships, be that customers, partners, suppliers, advisers or industry bodies. In addition, ensuring we have the right talent for the growth of our business and the financial resources in place at the right time to support that growth are key components of the CEO role.'

Roddy suppresses a yawn. He promised Lorraine he'd watch it to the end so he tries to concentrate. Cut to a change in location. Lorraine stands assertively. In the background is a brightly lit, sunny (lucky with the weather that morning!) and busy Galway docks. Synth and drum backbeat start up again. Slightly different tempo.

'People ask me how I prioritise and organise my working life. As we all know, most plans rarely survive first contact with market forces. For that reason, a realistic level of flexibility is necessary. However I like to maintain a prioritised mental map around customers, strategy execution or horizon scanning.'

Roddy presses pause on the YouTube video. Checks how many seconds are left. Nearly two minutes to run. He sighs and presses play. New locale. More of a close-up. Darker background. Lorraine appears frighteningly determined.

'All businesses face challenges going forward. But we at Zeitgeist Technologies like to tackle them head on. The ever-changing landscape of technological innovation introduces freshly evolving scenarios. The challenge becomes how to integrate these changed circumstances and advances into the world of business to give our customers a competitive advantage and, at the same time, setting realistic expectations and minimising risk.'

He pauses the video again. He just can't take any more. He turns it off and wonders, what do Lorraine Abigail Heuston and himself actually have in common?

The American rock critic and cultural commentator Zak Calhoun – five failed marriages – once remarked that legendary bluesman BB King's two greatest songs sum up the path of every relationship. Things start off with 'Rock Me Baby' but end up with 'The Thrill is Gone'. Roddy and Lorraine, at this stage, after thirteen years together, are somewhere approaching 'The Thrill is Gone.'

Obviously, there are the money issues. There has been an alarming discrepancy in their earning power since he became a trailblazing practitioner of short-term contract work over the last ten years. He does insist, though, that he is a godsend when a handyman has to call. He spends hours waiting in the house for electricians or plumbers or tilers to turn up. Does she ever give him credit for that? No. Of course when the handyman eventually does arrive, two hours late – 'traffic was a killer this morning' – the first thing he says to Roddy is 'Off work this morning, are you?' Goddamned inquisitive handymen! Why do they presume everyone is working... all of the time? Have they never heard of a career break? To reconfigure one's long-term priorities? To pursue one's creative dreams? To try and locate one's inner Jim Carrey? No. They are handymen. Mere mortals. Not potential orchestral conductors of the funny bone.

Roddy himself has done his best, in the past few weeks, to be useful around the house, despite not having an innate aptitude for DIY. Lorraine has been stoically supportive about those bookshelves (short-lived) he constructed in their living room just before Christmas. And she did drive him to A&E to get that tetanus shot, after that unfortunate mishap with hammer and nail.

In all honesty, though, Lorraine still isn't completely sold on his plans about a career in comedy.

'You spend your whole day sitting at home watching George Carlin DVDs.'

'It's research.'

'It's sitting on your arse doing nothing.'

'I'm studying technique.'

'You're studying the technique of sitting on your arse all day doing nothing.'

'It might give me some ideas. For constructing jokes.'

'Look it pet, all I know is you made a big deal a few months back about your so-called Comedy Covenant, and I agreed to go along with it. We've even held on to last year's blood smudged calendar when it was time to throw it out. But it's now the middle of January. You've only got nine months left. In business and in life Roddy, deadlines should be adhered to.'

She kisses him on the head.

'Remember now, I'm not giving out. I'm just explaining.'

Sometimes Roddy believes himself and Lorraine are a case of opposites detracting. She is solutions-based. Always suggesting that he 'up his skill-set'. He is delusions-based. Still wrapping himself around the belief, at the age of forty-three, that wanting something to happen means it's going to happen.

Then there are the misunderstandings. The time a few years back when they visited Agnes and she gave Lorraine a jacket to congratulate her on setting up Zeitgeist Technologies. It was a jacket Agnes wore back in 1989. The cast of *Dynasty* would have considered those shoulder pads excessive.

Roddy was so embarrassed. Agnes is always trying to pass off her cast offs on Lorraine. 'Oh, that looks lovely on you,' Agnes had said. 'Oh, thank you,' Lorraine replied politely. It is important to stress at this stage that Lorraine is five foot nine. Tall and slim. Agnes is five foot one. Short and squat. Tall and slim. Short and squat. Tall and slim. Short and squat. Maybe if it was repeated regularly enough it might enter his mother's head. The clothes can never fit!!!! Leaving aside the taste and ho-hum quality of the fare on offer. But Lorraine was too nice to say these things so pretended to like the jacket. Then Agnes called Roddy into the room where herself and Lorraine were and said 'Isn't that lovely on Lorraine?' Roddy looked at Lorraine and Lorraine nodded approvingly at him. And Roddy replied 'It is lovely.' Because Roddy believed Lorraine really did like it. He didn't know she was pretending. Roddy thought, 'Well, at least she finally likes something mother has given her.'

Of course, on the journey home, Lorraine asked, 'Why did you say it was lovely on me?

It's a joke. It's awful.' And Roddy replied, 'Well, I thought you liked it. You nodded approvingly.' Lorraine retorted, 'Well, I couldn't hurt your mother's feelings. I couldn't very well say, me tall and slim, you short and squat.' 'Let's give it to Oxfam,' Roddy had suggested. Lorraine's insecurity took over, 'What happens if she expects me to wear it, next time I see her?' Roddy assured her Agnes would forget because she is getting old. However, during a phone call quite recently, out of the blue, Agnes had inquired, 'Is Lorraine still wearing that jacket I gave her? It looked positively wonderful on her.' Roddy decided not to share this jacket news update with Lorraine. But he did wonder and still wonders how two people can spend all this time living together and have no idea what each other is thinking.

There are other issues.

The ongoing disagreements about Roddy's tendency to embrace the life of a hermit. Roddy is wedded to his unsociable nature. His habits and routines. In fact, he is answerable to, as he calls it, Mr. Routine. Roddy and the passive aggressive Mr. Routine are always arguing. And Mr. Routine, mostly, comes out on top.

One recent Tuesday night, Lorraine 'on the

spur of the moment' had asked him if he wanted to go to the cinema. This totally threw him. He had to confer with Mr. Routine.

'Lorraine wants to go to the cinema tonight.'

'You can't go,' Mr. Routine replied.

'Why not?' Roddy wondered.

'Because you never go to the cinema Tuesday night. Anyway you were all set to sit in with me and watch television. The news at nine. Then the weather forecast at nine-twenty-five. Despite the fact that we've already watched it at five-to-seven.'

Sometimes, Roddy wants to break free. But he is trapped. He recalls an old Dryden quote he came across during his time in college – 'First we make our habits, then our habits make us'. He longs to 'be spontaneous' but he accepts Mr. Routine has a very strong hold over him.

Only on a rare occasion is Mr. Routine a little more flexible if he is given at least a week's notice of Roddy and Lorraine's intended plans.

But more often than not those planned evenings don't work out at this stage. Take last month. That dinner party at their friends Philip and Majella's house where Roddy and Lorraine had brought a bottle of Pernod Ricard to give to their hosts, which they themselves had received a few years back as a present. And just as they were about to ring Philip and Majella's doorbell they remembered that it was actually Philip and Majella who had given them the bottle of Pernod Ricard. Probably *they* had got it from yet *another* couple and wondered, what do we do with this bottle of Pernod Ricard? Give it to Roddy and Lorraine.

Roddy insisted that Philip and Majella wouldn't remember. Lorraine contested that they would remember. So Roddy and Lorraine had to scamper off and find an off-licence, in the pouring rain, in an area they were unfamiliar with. Poisonous recriminations were flung back and forth with abandon. Dogs barked at them. And attacked one of them. (Guess who?) Youths in hoodies sniggered at them. Eventually they found an off-licence but Lorraine wasn't happy with the wine selection. She didn't want Philip and Majella to think they lacked taste by bringing only a ten euro bottle of Rioja. A sixteen euro bottle was required. At least. So they went looking elsewhere. Eventually they located another off-licence. They found a suitably priced bottle of red wine, a fine award-winning Cabernet Sauvignon from 2010, headed back to Philip and Majella's only to accidentally drop new present (bottle of Cabernet Sauvignon) and original present (bottle of Pernod Ricard) in transit.

All this of course is impacting on their sex life. Lorraine has become bored with their usual coital interaction and wants them to try some new things. She's become obsessed with trying out 'the kitchen worktop' position. She has seen it in all the movies. Hero brings his new girlfriend home. They enter his kitchen and while ripping each other's clothes off he hoists her on the kitchen worktop and effortlessly starts thrusting. This becomes ever more intense and leads to an ululating crescendo of carnal bliss. There are a few problems with the suggestion Roddy has tried to explain. Firstly, Mr. Routine won't be happy. There'll need to be a lot of explanation and advance warning.

But more importantly, there's another issue. Sadly, Roddy takes after Agnes in physique. 'Short and squat' will always find it very difficult, on a technical, practical and geometrical level, to do the 'kitchen worktop' position with 'tall and slim'.

AMBROSE HEGARTY, FARMER POET

'What's the latest? Any news with the comedy thing?'

Forthright farmer scribbler poet, Ambrose Hegarty, always gets straight to the point.

'To be honest, I haven't done much about it over the last while. There was Auntie Eileen's funeral, the trip away to New Orleans, then various bits and bobs, and then Christmas was upon us and that's always disruptive and I think we both agree that the comedy workshop a month or two back with Cormac Creedon...'

'The stop-off at the slurry pit of failure?'

'Yes... was a bit of a non-event.'

There is a pause. Roddy sighs.

'Maybe I'm too old already. Comedy is a young man's game. What was that Shakespeare line about Falstaff?'

Ambrose shrugs. Not a Bard of Avon completist. Roddy retrieves the quote from that couple of ill-fated years in college. Somnolence-inducing lectures in The O'Flaherty Theatre on Tuesday afternoons.

'How ill white hairs become a fool and jester.'

Ambrose is not impressed.

'But you don't have any white hairs, ya flippin' eejit. What are you on about?'

'I've a few grey ones now. Noticed them last week.'

'Grey hairs! White hairs! Cop on to yourself, will you. Hasn't hurt Steve Martin's career!'

Ambrose looks critically at Roddy.

'Excuses. Excuses. Excuses. God almighty, Roddy Bodkin, I've known you now for nearly twenty years. And the one thing you've always banged on about is how you'd love to try a bit of the auld stand-up comedy.'

Ambrose mutters to himself. Looks at Roddy.

'Did you ever hear of Gaudi?'

Roddy doesn't react. Ambrose continues.

'There was this fella Gaudi like, and he was an architect like, and he lived in Spain like, and he built these mad buildings like, and he was like a cartoonist except they were buildings like, and they were three-dimensional instead of drawings like, completely daft looking things, and he didn't take drugs or anything like, but he was quite religious like, and he started working on this church like in 1882 like, in Barcelona like, and jaysus he just kept adding to it like, but he could never finish it like, and people said to him, are you ever going to finish that auld church of yours, and he'd say I'm getting there, but jaysus didn't he walk out in front of a tram in 1926 and didn't he go and die and he never finished his bloody church and jaysus Christ they're still flippin' working on it to this very day. The Sagrada Familia it's called or some auld shite like that. Well, you talking about doing the comedy over the years is a bit like that, ya big feckin' eejit! Will ya stop talking about it and start doing the bloody thing, will ya?'

'Ambrose, I haven't been, totally, wasting my days. I've done the odd thing about it. It's more difficult than I thought, that's all. I rang Declan, the guy who books the open spots for The Róisín Dubh comedy nights, and he offered me the first open spot available. In late March...'

'Well done. Good man yourself. Something to work towards.'

'2015.'

'For flip sake.'

'So many people want to be comedians, nowadays.'

Roddy sighs. Orders two more pints. Roddy

and Ambrose are in their natural habitat. An ideal home for a little routine they've played out for years. 'How are you getting on?' one of them asks. 'I'm fine at the moment. I'm in a good place,' the other replies. Then, after a pause, they both say in unison 'A pub'. The pub is called PJ's in Lower Salthill and they spend many hours there imbibing and griping. Mainly griping. Galway – City of The Diatribes.

How did these two misfits meet? Like many a couple in Ireland, it was the drink that brought them together. A woman also has to be factored into the equation.

It was way back. Early summer. 1994. Kurt Cobain had recently found a 20-gauge shotgun that worked. Jack Charlton's Boys in Green were having a World Cup encore in America. Cinema audiences had just been introduced to Hugh Grant's awkward posh dithering in *Four Weddings and a Funeral*.

Also that June, Ambrose Hegarty fell in love. He had spotted a lithe auburn-haired beauty one Wednesday evening on the promenade of Salthill. This could be the one, he thought. He followed her as she entered a slightly run-down community centre. Stooping outside under an open window he caught a quick glimpse of her as she stood up and announced to the assembled gathering.

'My name is Donna and I'm an alcoholic.'

'Hi Donna!'

An AA meeting, Ambrose mused. A woman with a past. I like a woman with a past. I'd love a woman with a past in my future. Or a woman with *no* past in my future. Feck it – I'd just love a woman in my future. Her accent was northern. Belfast, perhaps. But how could he get closer to this woman? Already elevated after only six-hundred-and-four seconds to the status of Woman of His Dreams. He could frequent her place of work. But how could he find out where she was employed? He would have to secretly follow her home after the AA meeting, which is a bit dubious, hide outside her house overnight, dodgier still, and, keeping a discreet distance, trail her to her place of work the following morning. That's presuming she works. Maybe she doesn't have a job and is on the dole. Like most of the young people in Ireland in 1994 who haven't emigrated. What happens if she lives miles away in the middle of nowhere and she never leaves her house because she doesn't have a job and one of her neighbours spots him up a telegraph pole clinging awkwardly while looking through a pair of binoculars? The guards would be called. The whole thing would end in disaster before it had even begun. No, there was a simpler solution. He'd just have to join Alcoholics Anonymous and try to strike up a conversation with her the following week. But there was one problem. Up until that time, forthright farmer scribbler poet Ambrose Hegarty was an absolute teetotaller.

He would have to take up the drink. In order to give up the drink.

He started with a glass of shandy. In Lonergan's pub. A tentative experience. Hadn't yet acquired a taste. This would take time. But it would be worth it. For Donna. He didn't care what she'd got up to in the past. Probably an ex-IRA member. A honey trap for unsuspecting British soldiers. Mad into the Irish language. That *would* be a potential cause of friction but if she consented to have sex with him, regularly (even irregularly, he could live with that) and be a loving and supportive companion over the next thirty years, he could reluctantly endure such a fallacious cultural obsession. He was one of the few people born in Connemara who could not abide the Irish language. His parents, Paudie and Nonie, spoke it morning, noon and night when he was a child. He always wished they spoke French. That sounded *trés élégant*. But Irish? Bedouins gargling. When you speak Irish you sound like a Bedouin sheik gargling. He had heard some fella say that recently at a sparsely attended, inaugural anti-Irish language lobby group, For Focail Sake, meeting held at The Skeffington Arms Hotel on Eyre Square.

This fella worked in a travel agency, and had a virulent hatred of all things from Galway. And from Ireland. They had hit it off immediate-ly. Maybe he should get this fella – what was his name? Bodkin – yes that was the name, Bodkin, Roddy Bodkin (wonder was he any relation to long-dead Michael Bodkin, one of young Nora Barnacle's many ill-fated suitors?) to help start him drinking. But he hardly knew this Roddy Bodkin. Men just don't ring other men they hardly know and ask them to go out drinking. The other man might think there is an ulterior motive. In the back door shenanigans department. Now he was not a man to pass judgements – actually he *was* a man to pass judgements, constantly, every living moment of his day – but that sort of carry-on wasn't his cup of tea. And the very practice did complicate matters in the making of perfectly innocent phone calls between men.

He had another sip of the shandy. And grimaced as he swallowed. This was hopeless. He would never be able to drink this alcohol stuff. He'd just have to go to the meeting next week and pretend.

The following Wednesday night Ambrose turned up at the Alcoholics Anonymous meeting in Salthill. Donna was there. A pony-tailed goddess in denim. He was nervous. But, so what if he lied? Who'd know? Fergus Molloy, that's who. Ambrose had spotted him near the front. He'd been part of Ambrose's social circle a few years back. Semi-circle. Never really a complete circle. Pub quizzes and what not. Maximum four fellas. Pimple MacNicol, who's married now in Australia, Thesaurus O'Reilly who runs a betting shop in Abbeyknockmoy and The Eejit Atkins who's still on the run. Fergus knew Ambrose had never touched a drop. This could be trouble. But, maybe Fergus wouldn't say anything. He was always a likeable fella. Fergus is sound as a bell, the others would say. No flies on Fergus. Sound man, Fergus. Not a bother on Fergus. Steady as she goes, Fergus. There's sound and there's sound but there is no one sounder than Fergus. Sound. Sound as a bell, like. That's Fergus.

The meeting commenced. Two new participants, Billy – Hi Billy! and Marie Louise – Hi Marie Louise!, briefly chronicled their stories. Then Daniel, the chairman, noticing the fidgeting third newcomer of the evening, gestured towards Ambrose. Ambrose sighed tensely. He looked nervously at the ever-radiant Donna and stood up.

'My name is Ambrose, and I'm an alcoholic.'

The in-unison 'Hi Ambrose!' was interrupted by an outburst from behind.

'Will you go away out of that! I've never seen you with a drink in your life, Ambrose Hegarty!' It was Fergus Molloy.

Ambrose protested.

'I am Fergus. I am an alcoholic.'

'You are not.' Fergus persisted. 'Red Lemonade is your favourite drink. Or Club Orange. Or if you are feeling a bit wild and crazy you might have a Seven-Up. How dare you offend us hardened drinkers by coming in here and saying you're an alcoholic.'

'I'm a secret drinker,' Ambrose stated. Clutching at (soft drink) straws.

'Will you ever go and feck off with you and your secret drinking.'

Still standing, Ambrose suddenly felt light-headed and nauseous. The other AA members were becoming restless. He glanced over at a puzzled Donna. Daniel the chairman, attempting to calm things, adjourned the meeting for a few minutes. After a small chat with an increasingly none-too-convincing Ambrose, Daniel thought it best Ambrose re-examine his options, give it a few weeks, and return if he still felt he really needed the support of Alcoholics Anonymous.

On his way home that evening, Ambrose was livid. I'll drink day and night just to prove it to those feckers! I'll get cirrhosis of the liver just to prove it to those feckers!

The thirst for revenge overcame any possible misunderstanding and embarrassment on the whole *maybe this guy phoning me is gay like and wanting to go out with me* angle. He decided to finally ring Roddy.

'Is that Roddy. Roddy Bodkin? Howye, this is Ambrose. Ambrose Hegarty. I'm one of the members of For Focail Sake.'

'Oh. Howye Ambrose.'

'Listen, do you want to meet up for a couple of jars?'

There was a pause. As Ambrose had feared, while Roddy debated a response he started having his own private doubt-ridden debate. Why does this fella Ambrose *really* want to meet up? I hardly know him. Irish men don't usually ring unexpectedly wanting to go for a drink if you've only met them once or twice. A woman might with another woman. Yes. Women are different. But a man. Never. I hear they do so on the continent. Even go for meals together. Have a bottle of wine together. Share jokes and laugh over a three-course dinner at a restaurant together. Discuss Football and the films of Luis Buñuel. Even embrace when they part. And no one pays them a bit of notice. But *here*? It doesn't work that way here. It has to be casual, like. Or you have to see them around, like. From work, like. Or they are just in the pub, like. Always, like. That's how you find a drinking companion. Never a phone call. That means there is an ulterior motive.

The pause became longer. Then Ambrose shouted down the line.

'Jaynee mackers, Roddy, this is all perfectly innocent. I swear. No funny business. I just want to go for a drink.'

The matter clarified, Roddy agreed to meet Ambrose the following evening.

Once Roddy was given a detailed outline of the predicament Ambrose faced, he offered to help. In those more irresponsible bygone days when drink driving was mandatory and trying to get into the *Guinness Book of Records* was often mistaken for a pint-drinking competition, Roddy felt absolutely no qualms about his decision.

A drinking schedule was devised. Four nights a week. First off, Roddy issued a non-shandy edict like a good coach eliminating bad habits from the beginning. Roddy insisted Ambrose had glasses of lager while he, Roddy downed pints of Guinness. This lasted for two weeks and then – a landmark date, Sunday July 10th 1994 – Ambrose had his first full pint.

Roddy was very proud of Ambrose and immediately bought him another one.

Three weeks later Ambrose, like a young athlete of promise, was quickly catching up with his mentor and was able to knock back three pints of Guinness during an evening session. There had been a few moments of tension – none more so than that near break-down of the whole intensive programme ten days previously when Ambrose had wondered aloud whether to ask for one or two drops of blackcurrant juice on his very first pint of Guinness – Roddy had stood up and announced solemnly, 'Do that, and I'm walking. There are certain things a drinks coach cannot countenance in any circumstances!'

Friday 12th August 1994. A further benchmark was achieved. After four pints of Guinness, Ambrose had been given a whiskey chaser. Up for any challenge and prepared to overcome any obstacle put before him, he knocked it back in one gulp.

The following evening, Roddy was out in the sea port village of Kinvara visiting Ger and Agnes who had moved there, from Salthill, the previous year. Ambrose felt he needed to sustain the progress made. Maintain a level of stamina. Keep that liver exercised. He decided to go into a pub. Alone. Five hours later he was pissed as a coot. His very first time. The more pissed he got, the more exotic-sounding drink he ordered. As a game.

After quaffing a second Frisky Mongoose he realised something. *This feels fucking great!* He rang Roddy in Kinvara to relate the news. A clearly baffled Agnes addressed her elder son from the hallway. 'Roddy dear, it's one of *your* friends.'

As day follows night, hangovers follow drunkenness. *This feels fucking awful!* Roddy told him not to worry. And mentioned some bizarre concept of a canine attacking you, and you having to chase it and cut off its tail and then consume it. Or something like that. Ambrose realised his cognitive ability was probably still drink-impaired during that late-morning advisory phone call.

The days went by. The months went by. Ambrose found he had a natural talent and constitution for drinking. But he wasn't alone. Galwegians love to drink. It's weather-related, Roddy put forward as a reason, a month or two later during the formal winding down of the short-lived For Focail Sake. That blanket of bleak that passes itself off as the sky. Eleven months of the year. The sky over Galway is a jigsaw puzzle of dark grey, assembled on a tablecloth of light blue, with two pieces missing. It's the opening credits of *The Simpsons* except the sky is darker and the clouds never really part to reveal music and brightness. Then there is the Galway rain. Unending moist discharges from the Atlantic. Or on other days, the deceptive thick drizzle that gradually soaks you like a slow-motion car wash without the suds. Healthier to stay indoors and ruin your insides than go out in *that*. Ambrose looked up from his barstool as yet another deluge arrived. Maybe all this drinking is a post-famine howl of anguish, Roddy then proffered as another reason for Galway's love of alcohol. Ambrose raised an eyebrow. Roddy continued. We are still drowning our sorrows for our long-dead starving antecedents. Ambrose thought about what Roddy had said for a moment. Sounds good enough to me. Another pint?

Three years later Ambrose Hegarty, now forthright farmer scribbler poet Ambrose Hegarty after having a few poems published in *New Western Writing*, was sitting at the bar in Ward's in Lower Salthill. It was teatime and with all this, relative, literary success he was busy fashioning himself on being a perfect blend of Dylan Thomas, Oliver Reed and a Pogues-at-their-peak Shane MacGowan. He'd already had five pints and was waiting for his friend Roddy Bodkin.

Suddenly he heard a Belfast accent order two mineral waters. A female Belfast accent. It was Donna. He'd forgotten all about her. But there she was. Still as luminous as ever. Still in denim. She looked at him. Tried to remember who he was. But couldn't. She paid for the drinks and took the two mineral waters and returned to her table. Sitting next to her was Fergus sound-as-a-fucking-bell Molloy. Ambrose got up from his stool. He staggered over to them. Evidently, now a love-struck couple. All snuggly-wuggly in the corner. He swayed in front of their table for a moment.

He slowly pointed at Fergus, but before speaking burped a little, then suddenly vomited over their drinks. Exorcist-style. Fergus and Donna recoiled in horror. Ambrose lurched to one side.

'I showed you! Showed you *all*! Who's the alcoholic now?'

He began to laugh hysterically, then suddenly losing his footing, fell over on his technicolour chunder.

A PROPOSAL OF MARRIAGE 2013

It is February 2013. Lorraine Heuston and Roddy Bodkin have already been together for thirteen years. It's fork in the road time. Full-time commitment and marriage or go their separate ways? Sometimes, Lorraine thinks she can do better, *much better*, but other times she thinks, better the woeful-at-DIY-and-at-other-things devil you know. Also, what about all those shared moments over nearly a decade and a half? Some, not perfect, but shared all the same. Lodged forever in the memory bank of the heart.

Roddy thinks if it's not broke why fix it? (That antipathy to DIY kicking in again.) Or even, if it *is* broke a little bit, why fix it? (Ditto.) Let things go on the way they've always been. Anyway, long-term couples who finally tie the knot have a huge divorce rate and most seem to break up within a year.

Meanwhile... destiny plays the trickster.

It's Valentine's Day. Former Galway minor hurling star and winner of the Connacht Young Entrepreneur of the Year Award 2009, Colm

Keady, enters Simply Chocolate, a newly opened upmarket chocolate boutique shop on Mainguard Street and purchases a Valentine's Heart made of Dark Chocolate Surprise from Teresa behind the counter. He places a ring and card inside. The card, printed in a special romantic font reads 'Will You Marry Me?' He then has the Dark Chocolate Surprise Valentine's Heart placed in a box and wrapped.

Colm drives to the family home of girlfriend, Sue Costello, in Spiddel, for a surprise pop-the-question visit. He is let in by Sue's mother, Ursula. To his disappointment, Sue is not in and after a slightly tense cup of tea with Ursula, Colm decides to leave. He picks up the wrapped present to take with him but a forceful Ursula intervenes.

'Arey, sure what are you taking that away with you for, sure you'll only have to bring it back again. Leave it with me here. I'll give it to her. She'll be thrilled.'

Colm, despite his illustrious career on the hurling fields of Carna and his ice-cool decision-making abilities as a very promising entrepreneur, is suddenly overcome by a lack of assertiveness. He leaves without the package.

A few hours later a radiant Sue returns home.

Ursula shows her the package. Sue opens it, looks at the chocolate heart and sighs. Doesn't like dark chocolate. Doesn't he *know* that? Men! She likes light chocolate, not as healthy, but that is what she prefers. Without opening the actual chocolate heart, Sue decides to rewrap it, accompany Ursula into town for some late afternoon shopping, and return the package. Teresa is on her break when Sue enters Simply Chocolate, and another sales girl, Holly, happily replaces the Dark Chocolate Surprise Valentine's Heart for a Light Chocolate Delight one.

That evening, Roddy and Lorraine watch *My Favourite Wife*, an old romantic comedy movie from 1940 with Cary Grant and Irene Dunne, in their living room in Whitestrand Avenue. Afterwards, Lorraine brings up the marriage topic, telling Roddy that, maybe, after all this time, they should tie the knot. She is a successful woman who runs her own company. He has a more nebulous life plan, that is true, but she loves him, likes the stability they give each other and, despite their intermittent disagreements and differing approaches to things, she would like them to make things permanent. Roddy sighs and asks why the hurry? Lorraine shakes her head and becomes reflective.

An anti-climactic pall hangs over the remainder of the evening.

Meanwhile, having gone past the end of his tether hours previously and unable to wait any longer, Colm rings Sue. He asks her if she liked her present. She replies she loved it. He asks her was that a 'yes'? She replies, yes, she loved the present. He persists and asks vaguely about 'the other thing'. She is confused, and wonders what 'other thing'? Despondent, Colm takes this as a negative and tells Sue he'll call her the next day.

In a deflated and very depressed state, Colm goes to The Goal Post bar in Wood Quay. Being a former hurling star who wore the maroon jersey with such pride and now a young and innovative entrepreneur, he is popular amongst the clientele and ends up getting very drunk and picking up a floozie from Kilfenora called Florrie. They go back to his place and have drunken dirty sloppy sex.

The following morning, Roddy is in town. He passes Simply Chocolate, decides to go inside, and buys a greatly reduced Dark Chocolate Surprise Valentine's Heart as a peace offering for Lorraine. He has it wrapped.

In the meantime, a perky Sue rings the doorbell of Colm's place. Florrie the floozie opens the door. Colm, half-dressed and groggy, comes out. When Sue sees him, she turns in disgust and leaves. Colm shouts after her but she doesn't respond. Filled with self-loathing and heartache, he curls up in a bundle on his new Hawaiian themed Futon and bawls like a baby. Florrie tries to locate her turquoise leggings.

That afternoon Roddy brings the wrapped package back to the house in Whitestrand Avenue. And he is wearing his black polo neck. As a further peace gesture. The black polo neck Lorraine had bought him on their first anniversary way back in 2001. She always liked men in black polo necks. Roddy thought he looked like a stunt man on holidays when he wore it. And he stopped wearing it soon afterwards. You don't wear the black polo neck any longer, she'd say. My neck is too small, he'd reply. But then like most men, as he approached his mid-thirties, suddenly his neck expanded. One night, a branch. The next morning, a tree trunk. And Lorraine would say to him, your neck is much fatter now, you can wear your black polo neck again.

He places the package on the kitchen table and later when Lorraine gets home, she smiles when she notices the package.

'For me?'

'For you.'

She unwraps the package. Dark chocolate. Her favourite! She then opens the Dark Chocolate Surprise Valentine's Heart and finds the ring and the printed card inside. She peers at the card. At first the kitschy sentimental print distracts her but she finally reads the words – 'Please marry me'.

She then holds up a ring and card.

Roddy's face turns albino ghost.

Lorraine looks at him for a moment. After gathering her thoughts but still quite happily stunned, she tells him he has taken her by complete surprise, especially after last evening, but that she loves the card and the ring and of course she'll marry him.

Albino ghost is incredulous.

'What?'

Lorraine starts a long monologue making plans for the marriage. Roddy looks on. He eventually tries to interject but is drowned out by Lorraine's rapid-fire enthusiasm.

Roddy thinks of the ice skater. The sexy ice skater in the skimpy outfit who slips in a big ice-skating championship while jiving to an up-tempo Strauss arrangement. She immediately gets up. Pretends she didn't fall. On the slight possibility the judges and those dwindling television viewers across Europe haven't noticed. But of course, they have noticed. Because you can't undo what is done.

Could Roddy undo what was done? Un-propose the marriage proposal. The marriage proposal he never made. He could. But there would be repercussions. Say if he tells her. It would all end. The meals. The staying-in. The comfy companionship. And how would Mr. Routine react to a complete break? He'd go into meltdown.

Roddy continues his calculations. He does have a good time with her. They do actually do the occasional thing together. And go to the occasional place together. Sure, they fight. Then they make up and have sex. Or try to have sex. Lorraine had promised 'the kitchen worktop position' was off the agenda for good, although she did mention something recently about 'the spontaneous garden shed manoeuvre'.

Generally, between them, things were goodish. Referencing BB King again, the thrill wasn't completely gone. Anyway, he's nearly forty-four. No spring chicken. Carrying a bit of weight, as they say. Does he really want to be out there again? Like one of those sad characters in an open leather jacket. Paunch bursting forth. Shirt buttons ready to pop. Drinking pints in some pub. Anxiously. Alone. While surveying the available 'talent'? Is he really going to find anyone better?

He hesitates over what to say next. Colour slowly reappears on his cheeks.

Then, Lorraine spots something while examining the back of the ring.

'From C. to S., with love. Strange. What does that mean?'

Roddy looks puzzled.

'Let me see.'

She looks at Roddy.

'What is this?'

Cheek colour disappears again. Roddy looks frazzled. She continues to query.

'Is the ring second-hand?'

Roddy looks alarmed. Reacts with faux innocence.

'What?'

Lorraine hands him the ring.

He examines it.

'Roddy, what is this? Who are C and S?'

'Eh. Just my luck getting the most short-sighted engraver working in a jewellery shop in Galway.'

She isn't amused by his quip.

'Where did you get this ring?'

'In the shop.'

She scrutinises him.

'What shop? That new chocolate boutique shop?'

There is a pause. She sighs.

'You take the biscuit Roddy Bodkin. You didn't know, did you? That the card and ring were in there, did you?'

'But I got you the chocolate Valentine's heart. A gesture of goodwill. Don't I get points for that? That other thing, granted, could be all a bit of a misunderstanding.'

Lorraine looks away.

'Oh God. I don't believe it. That's some other poor guy's engagement ring. Roddy, I think this whole thing, us, has been one long misunderstanding.'

DILEMMA FOR LORRAINE

Lorraine pees into a small lilac plastic bowl which had been used up to eight months previously for mixing corn flour, ground almond and organic butter, for that biscuit recipe that Roddy adored. She then places the home pregnancy test kit into the warm urine and waits for the required five seconds. She removes it and will now have to wait for two minutes as she observes the ticking seconds hand on her watch.

The baby would be Roddy's. But Roddy is history. That incident with the wedding ring was the final straw. OK, it wasn't his fault. In a way. But it shone a sharp, unforgiving light on their whole relationship. And where it was going. Nothing was ever going to change. If she meets someone new at some future date, he will have to be a driven, proactive, grown-up. He'll have to have some get up-and-go, not sit-down-and-stay. He'll have to be a maelstrom of activity. Not an immobile blob of inertia. Why did she stick with Roddy for so long? At the end of the day, he was just all talk and never evolved. When she first met him in 2000 in The Warwick, she was bowled over. She was young, twenty-three, lacking in confidence – he, eight years older, seemed so full of plans and energy and he had a sort of unique wit about him. Also they had been brought together by Ireland's most unlikely cupid, *Father Ted*. Over the years, so many Irish couples have been brought together after realising, on initial meeting, they share a favourite *Father Ted* episode. Roddy and Lorraine's favourite episode? The one with the Hairy Hands Syndrome where Jack is in The Home for Wayward Priests. By a mile. But as the years went on, and she grew older and developed, located her talents and found her own niche, Roddy seemed to get stuck. Become lethargic. Listless. And resigned.

Does she want a child? With the success of Zeitgeist Technologies? No. She'd have to take maternity leave. Forget that. And then when she goes back to work, the childminding costs would stack up. Still ludicrously expensive in this day and age. Tom and Eucharia could put in some shifts but come off it, fair is fair. Tadgh, Fiachra, Saoirse, Aonghus Óg, Brendan, Kasper and Muireann are more than enough grandchildren. Wait. She won't be pregnant. Stop catastrophizing, Lorraine. Anyway, if worse comes to worse, she could always get rid of it. Oh shit. She forgot. She lives in Ireland. 2013. Still reeling from the unnecessary death of poor, ill-fated Savita. Just down the road at the UHG. No, we don't do the 'a' word here. Women can do it elsewhere. Just not here. How many women give birth to unwanted children in Ireland because it is just too much effort to organise transport to, and accommodation in, London? All those secret phone calls. And appointments. Like something from a John Le Carré novel. To be honest, she doesn't know what she'll do. And then the Catholic guilt could kick in, if she went ahead with the termination, even if she hasn't been to church in twenty-five years.

Enough Lorraine! No Catholic guilt! If the test is positive she will ring her friend Martina in Birmingham. Maybe she could get it done there. Christ! Only seventeen seconds on the watch. Another minute and a half at least. How is it looking? Can she make out the plus or minus sign? Too soon to tell.

The actress Sarah Miles drinks her urine. So did Gandhi. People say it is a healthy thing to do.

Roddy Bodkin. Finally a father. She wouldn't tell him. Responsibility isn't really his strong suit. He wouldn't be interested, anyway. Roddy once told her that anytime, at awkward family gatherings or strained social situations, when some relative or stranger asks him in a low voice if he had any children – which is none of their business Roddy would emphasise, none of their fuckin' business – he tells them, no, because sadly he suffers from a rare medical disorder. Blue Semen Syndrome. That shuts the inquisitor up as they search, in a state of slight confusion and embarrassment, for the correct words of comfort. Roddy a dad? Not really his thing. As he says himself, he has no issue with 'no issue'. He once stated the only reason people have children is that there'll be somebody to do the reading at their funeral.

The second hand says thirty-four seconds. This is taking an age.

Lorraine's thoughts are suddenly interrupted when a roofer working on next-door's roof briefly steps past her bathroom skylight. Already preoccupied and jumpy, she accidentally kicks over the small bowl of urine.

'Holy fuck, shit!'

Frantically wiping the floor, and without thinking, she puts the inconclusive pregnancy test kit in the back pocket of her blue jeans. She then composes herself.

She walks out of the bathroom. A wasted pregnancy test kit. She should have bought that test kit double pack yesterday. Special offer. What was she thinking only buying the one? Which means another trip to Boots tomorrow.

She'll get a double pack tomorrow on her way to work, so if a similar situation occurs in the future and she wastes one, however unlikely, she can use the other one. Maybe she should always get a double pack from now on. How truly reliable are they? Say if the test kit that tells her she is not pregnant is faulty. Remember that old adage, a second opinion. She should always buy two. And do two tests. If both test results come out the same then everything is fine. But then again, there is a slight random possibility that maybe both of those test kits are faulty. Where does it end? Buy three? Four? Stop it, Lorraine! Roddy always told her she could be a bit neurotic sometimes. Maybe she is. Like that time a few months back in New Orleans. She was very happy with the hotel accommodation. But then she talked to a married couple in the elevator. They were not happy with their room. So she wondered if she was missing something to be unhappy about? Maybe their room wasn't as nice as she thought. Drove Roddy nuts.

Another day. Another pregnancy test.

This time a freshly scrubbed navy blue Tupperware object – more oblong shaped, less likely to be knocked over – which was used up to recently for Roddy's lunchtime sandwiches when he worked for Historical Walking Tours Galway.

She has bought four home pregnancy test kits. Two double packs. But promises only to use a maximum of two on this occasion. She listens out for any roofers. Nothing. They must have completed their work.

She finishes urinating and places the first test kit in the Tupperware for the required five seconds. Removes, checks her watch, notes the position of the seconds hand and waits.

What does she really feel about the possibility of being pregnant? She's too career-orientated and selfish. It would be like giving up five years of her life. Maybe she'll regret it down the line, maybe the biological clock will start clanging in a few years but she doesn't feel that way now and she's already nearly thirty-six. Not a scintilla of maternal instinct. As far as she's concerned all babies look like that comedy fella, from *Little Britain*, Matt Lucas, who annoys Roddy greatly.

It is later. Lorraine sits on the couch in the living

room, watching a mute flat-screen television and drinking a glass of red wine. She notices a stain on the cream rug beneath her. She has used up the four pregnancy test kits after all. Just to be sure. Won't need to pee for a week. Each time the result was the same. Negative. She feels relieved. A definite signal. Time to finally move on from Roddy Bodkin.

LONDON CALLING

The 1960s mystic and guru Osho Rajneesh once stated that all hatred is self-hatred. Obviously he'd never visited Galway. If he had, guaranteed he would have made a special geographical exemption to the above pronouncement.

Roddy hates Galway.

'How come?' ask acquaintances from around the country, who adore the place.

'How much time do you have?' Roddy replies before methodically going down his list.

The rain.

The corrosive parochialism.

The Irish language speakers.

The administrative incompetence.

The giant puppets with the enormous heads from those Macnas parades that regularly inhabit his most vivid nightmares.

The horrendous traffic.

The new buildings that use the cheapest light-coloured exteriors that will look mouldy and damp within a year.

The locals who use platitudes like 'he's one of

our own' or 'he's never forgotten his roots'.

Roddy doesn't want to be one of their own and he'd gladly forget his roots. The last thing he ever wants to be known as is 'a Galway man through and through'.

To be fair, it isn't just Galway Roddy detests. That whole area around Galway he finds problematic. That whole largish area. South of Galway to Cork. East of Galway to Dublin. North of Galway to Belfast. Come to think of it, he'd love to ask Osho Rajneesh to add some extra geographical exemptions to that theory on hatred. Or, better still, why not go the whole hog and make all of Ireland exempt?

After the recent final split with Lorraine – things never recovered after those unfortunate events with the chocolate egg – and his now fluid accommodation situation, (four days at Ronan's – purgatory, two days at Ambrose's – hell) this seems the ideal time to finally leave his cursed hometown and begin afresh somewhere new. Most importantly it will give him an opportunity to begin belatedly adhering to the Comedy Covenant. The clock is still ticking, after all. Only two-hundred-and-fourteen days until September 30th.

Forcefully dismissing Mr. Routine's persistent

protests, he has booked a flight to the comedy capital of the world.

London.

A month later. London doesn't seem like such a great idea, either. It's like a bigger version of Galway. Dirty. Damp. Depressing. And the beer is worse. There are also, ominously, some Irish language speakers, but Roddy has promised himself never to frequent McGuerty's bar in Cricklewood again.

He is staying with old school friend Noel Sugrue and his wife Jane in Wood Green. Over the years they had continually invited him to London, to try out 'the comedy thing', during their visits back to Galway, but those visits had become less frequent once Turlough and Deirdre, the twins, were born in 2003. And Roddy detected a slight surprise in Noel's reaction when he did finally turn up at number thirty-two Hastings Road, holding a beige travel bag and looking for a place to stay.

'Just for a few days. Until I've found my feet. I've already got a couple of possible gigs lined up. Don't want to impose.'

'No problem, my man. Putting on the pounds, huh? '

The first few days have flown by. Old school

stories have been exhumed. Wine has been opened. Children have been fawned over. Television has been watched. And now, a certain pattern to the days has emerged.

Roddy leaves most mornings after Noel and Jane have left the kids off to school and ends up going to a coffee shop down the road. He buys *The Guardian* and nurses a large cappuccino. For three hours. Staring purposefully at his call-and-text-only Nokia mobile phone on the light blue Formica surface, he contemplates making a few tentative inquiries to venue owners but defers things. Excuses always at hand. They're probably on their eleven o'clock break. They're probably on an early lunch break. They're probably not back from their lunch break. They've probably knocked off work early. They're probably not working there anymore. They're probably dead.

Some days he longs to go into London City centre but money is tight, so he ends up sitting in the inner courtyard of a nearby shopping mall, next to some exhausted afternoon shoppers. And observes. A crow picks at the square of Kit-Kat chocolate on the footpath. A guy with the look of a 1950s Teddy boy adjusts his hair using the back of a CD as a mirror. An old woman furtively raids a plastic bag and eats some biscuits. Some young schoolgirls improvise a hip-hop dance movement.

He really should have assembled more comedy material before he left Galway. The only stuff he has is a bit Ambrose penned about something Ambrose calls 'fierce conundrums'. It isn't bad but limited in scope. If only he could come up with some stuff of his own.

Other occasions in London he gets on the Tube. Goes on the Piccadilly line from Wood Green to Cockfosters. Just because he finds the name Cockfosters hilarious. There is nothing much in Cockfosters so sometimes he just turns around and *fuck the expense* goes straight into Leicester Square. Staring at his reflection as the train hurtles through the bowels of this great metropolis, he marvels at how quickly he's become just another Irish man at a loose end in London. He thinks of his Uncle Paddy. His father's oldest brother. Lost in that London-Irish Community Centre twilight zone for the last fifty years. In 1960, Uncle Paddy wore a pair of spectacles that made him look like a playwright or a nuclear physicist. But Paddy was a navvy. And hated English people. Because they all called him Paddy. 'But it's your name, Paddy,' family members would tell him on his visits home. 'Beside the point. It's the *way* they say it.'

When in London City centre Roddy spends his hours eating in cheap Chinese restaurants on Charing Cross Road. Or just walking. He notices most shows advertised in the West End seem to be a theatrical rehashing of something that has already been a success as a film or an adaptation of a best-selling book.

It is the following week. A slightly stressed Jane knocks on the door of the guest bedroom.

'Roddy, I'm not putting pressure on you, and don't feel that I am, but any news yet? Any sign of those gigs and the ball starting to roll?'

'No news yet. The one I had this week was cancelled. But there are others in the pipeline, I can assure you.'

Roddy is beginning to feel the increased tension in *chez* Sugrues. The kids are beginning to find him an inexplicable intrusion and Jane is starting to give him the evil eye. With both eyes.

In retrospect, Roddy has never totally clicked with Jane. She was always his friend Noel's girlfriend. And later, wife. Roddy believes that the spouses of friends are like a get-one-for-free deal. That extra element to the equation you are really not that pushed about.

One evening he decides to get out of the house for a few hours and ends up in the local comedy club. Saturday night at The Comedy Hut. Why didn't he think of this earlier? Ordering a beer, and sitting at the back to avoid being picked on by MC Keith Hunt, over a two-hour show he laughs just the once, when deadpan comedian with the crazy hair, Marcus Haddock – Half human! Half fish! – delivers the line, 'I was once in a band called Luminous Acne. We were good in spots.' All the other acts seem to end each punchline by asking wazatallabout? The punters appear to love it. Wazatallabout? However, Roddy is confused and alarmed by one thing. Keith Hunt keeps shouting 'give it up' as each performer departs the stage. It takes a while for him to understand that Keith isn't offering every act brutally blunt career advice but just asking the audience to applaud and cheer them on.

Overall, it is an enjoyable evening, the place is buzzing and Roddy is energised and doesn't feel intimidated by the atmosphere. He thinks to himself, I could be as funny as that! Fortified by a small 'large' whiskey – those criminally modest English spirit portions, perfidious bloody Albion! – he approaches Keith Hunt afterwards. Keith is friendly and chatty.

'Fifty quid for twenty minutes. Top of the bill Steve Class gets a hundred and twenty quid, but as his poster says, he *is* class. But comedy is not that easy. A cruel and fickle mistress. She can laugh at you, not with you. Or just fucking ignore you! Don't get nuffink for nuffink in this business. Got to do a few open spots first. Do five minutes, see if you got what it takes. I'm looking for open spots at the moment, the club just started three weeks ago. I've got another one opening in Boston Manor next month. People say Keef, you're taking on too much, I say, listen mate, as long as I've got my elf. Your elf is your welf, innit? I can open as many bleeding clubs as I want. Anyway, people will always want to laugh! I'll put your name down for next Thursday night, owright? About five minutes? If you're any good, I can put you down for a half spot in a few weeks, where you'd do about ten minutes. There'd be a couple of quid in it. They always like Irish blokes. So what's your name?'

'Roddy Bodkin.'

Keith laughs.

'Good name. It's got a certain ring to it. It sort of flows. Roddy Bodkin. I like it. Yeh. Be here around eight. See you, mate.'

Suddenly the future looks less bleak for Roddy. Imagine having three or four gigs a week. He could move out of Noel and Jane's place. Find a flat of his own.

Who knows where all this could lead. He's read about these comedy club open spots. One week a guy is working on an oil-rig, gets up and tells a few jokes, and by the following year he has his own television show. London is a vast land of opportunity. If you can make it there you can make it anywhere. Even New York. Wait a minute. Hold those horses. Yes. Best to take one step at a time, for now, and keep the feet firmly on the ground. Because most importantly, some blisteringly funny shit-hot comedy material needs to be written.

The following morning, he pops his head into the kitchen.

'I'm heading off now. Have a definite gig on the horizon.'

A relieved Jane and Noel look at each other. With a spring in his step, Roddy leaves with a small notebook and biro tucked confidently in his jacket pocket and heads to the coffee shop with the light blue Formica surfaces. He orders his large cappuccino. And removes a sheet of paper from his other jacket pocket. He tries reading Ambrose Hegarty's child-like scrawl.

'When you tie the lace of one shoe, almost immediately, you always have to tie the lace of the other shoe. Explain that fierce conundrum.'

Ah, that would be his catch-phrase – explain that fierce conundrum – it will make him different from all those 'wazatallabout' comedians. He sighs. He is concerned about the dearth of other non-Ambrose material. But he still has a few days before the gig to finesse a few quarter-formed ideas of his own.

A few evenings later, having put the twins to bed, an exhausted Jane and Noel sit down at the dinner table with Roddy. Jane looks at Noel. Noel speaks.

'So, how are things?'

'That gig I mentioned. It's on in The Comedy Hut tomorrow night.'

They look surprised. Then become supportive.

'Oh. That's great.'

Roddy pauses. He looks down. He smiles weakly. He pauses again. Then he has an idea. With a captive audience in front of him – granted only two – why not try out some of Ambrose's 'fierce conundrum' material. He looks at Jane and Noel.

'Want to hear some stuff?'

'Sure.'

He unfolds the sheet of paper. At this stage he has developed a feel for Ambrose Hegarty's, ahem, comic voice. Roddy clears his throat. And speaks.

'Why is it that when you see someone with a beard and he's had it for years and then one day he shaves it off, you think to yourself, he looks different. Whereas, if he was clean-shaven all his life, and one day he decided to grow a beard and a few weeks later you see him with a fully grown beard, you just think to yourself, oh, he's grown a beard. So if he hasn't had the beard for years and then he grows one that's alright but if he's had the beard all the time and then he shaves it off, that's not alright. Explain that fierce conundrum.'

Despite a distinct lack of response, Roddy decides to continue.

'It's the same with the fella and the guitar. If you're used to seeing a fella onstage with a guitar and then one day you see him singing without the guitar – jeez you get an awful shock. But jeez, if he never uses the guitar in the first place and then he decides in the middle of the concert to go over and pick up a guitar, you can handle that, no bother. Explain that fierce conundrum.'

Roddy tousles his hair nervously. Jane looks at Noel. Roddy coughs but ploughs on.

'You know when you haven't bitten your tongue for about four months and then you bite it – what happens? Within five minutes you bite it in the exact same spot again. Explain that fierce conundrum.'

Still nothing that could be qualified as a response.

Feeling ill-at-ease, Roddy then accidentally bites his tongue.

There is a long pause. Then Noel turns to Jane.

'Is that series with Sarah Lancashire finishing up tonight?'

'Yeh. It's just starting. I think it began at nine. Roddy, do you want to come in and watch it?'

Chastened by what has just happened, Roddy nods. Then he accidentally and forcefully bites his tongue. Again. In the exact same spot.

When Roddy Bodkin was nine he played soccer in an under-10 league in his local parish of Salthill. He loved it at first. He was doing well. He was on the team. Played out on the wing. But then he caught a bad dose of whooping cough. He was out sick for a few weeks. Fully recuperated he turned up the following month to find his place on the team had been taken by Theo Logan. From then on he would go to the training sessions, practice with the other boys but once match day arrived Theo would always get the nod from Mr. Lally, the coach. Roddy became disenchanted. He grew tired of going to the training sessions. With no prospect of getting any game time he started skipping them. He would leave home pretending to attend but would just cycle around for two hours. He had no perseverance. He didn't fight for his place. He didn't compete with Theo Logan. He just threw in the towel. Accepted that this is the way it is from now on. No point trying to change things. Get out while you're behind!

Roddy thinks of Theo Logan as he sits in the bar across the road from The Comedy Hut. It is Thursday night. Five-to-eight. He finishes his drink. And analyses his quickly approaching standup debut. Ambrose's material needs work. A lot of work. He can't go on tonight. He needs more time. Why start off on the wrong footing? He knows Cormac Creedon told them at the comedy workshop to take whatever gig you get. But Cormac Creedon wasn't working with Ambrose Hegarty's 'fierce conundrum' material. He'll be crucified over there at The Comedy Hut. No. He just needs a little bit more time to work things out. Just another week or two.

One afternoon, the following week, Roddy is walking up Hastings Road.

A taxi-man pulls up and asks him for directions to number thirty-two. Roddy points and says straight ahead, then take a left. The taxi-man drives on. Roddy is puzzled.

'Wonder what Noel and Jane want a taxi for?'

Roddy turns the corner and sees Jane at the front door of the house. The taxi-man is packing a beige travel bag into the boot. A familiar travel bag. *His* travel bag. He approaches Jane. She sighs.

'Sorry Roddy. Noel is away on a work trip and I decided to take matters into my own hands. Maybe it's best if you go back to the auld sod until you're fully committed to whatever you want to do. I got you this. Think of it as a farewell present.'

She hands him an airline ticket.

'It's very difficult to settle in London. It's a big place. Anyway, Roddy, I always see you as a Galway man through and through.'

MEMORIES OF HOME

Roddy has been back from London for three weeks. The day of the return journey he was greeted by a torrential downpour, almost on cue, after the bus passed through Ballinasloe – what his Dublin-based Uncle Charlie used to refer to as 'the welcoming committee', during frequent visits west in the 1980s. 'Not a drop of rain all the way to Athlone, then the feckin' welcoming committee showed up in force.'

Roddy is temporarily staying with Agnes in Kinvara. On his way home he'd read something of interest in *The Irish Times*. In 1959 Jean-Paul Sartre visited the house of American film director John Huston in Craughwell, County Galway, to work on a screenplay about Sigmund Freud. The same Sigmund Freud who had stated that the Irish were the one race impervious to psychoanalysis. The collaboration between Jean-Paul Sartre and John Huston was not a success. Of his stay in Galway, Sartre telegraphed Simone De Beauvoir and said 'I can't say I'm bored. It's worth living through this once.'

Trouble is, Roddy is bored and he's already lived through this once. During the first half of his life. And now he has returned. Tail between his legs. Living at home again with a parent.

Teatime with Agnes is always the same. Heated up gruel. Four day old gruel. Old people, more susceptible to picking up bugs and fatal diseases, seem much more cavalier about eating old gruel. Is it because they don't care anymore? Their sense of taste has gone? Or because they are mean? His parents' generation never threw anything away and the feeling of quiet satisfaction from finishing four-day-old gruel is greater for mother than the worry of picking up food poisoning leading to eventual extinction. Strange where people's priorities lie. And whatever happened to mother's eyebrows? They seem to be randomly crawling higher and higher each day. Like two pissed earwigs.

'Roddy, did you talk to Catriona about getting Tessie's number?'

'I did.'

'It's only a small job, but it'll take your mind off your London disappointment.'

'My London experience.'

'Alright, whatever you want to call it. '

Despite the complete calamitous nature of his

sojourn, by the end of his stay in London, something very odd began to happen to Roddy. He had started to have slightly warmer feelings towards Ireland. For starters being in Blighty reminded him that *his* country of birth never invaded anywhere else. And subjugated and exploited other peoples. And plundered the greatest cultural artefacts from these countries to exhibit in famous museums. Although, to be honest, the Irish would have been truly incompetent colonisers. The only legacy they'd have left behind would have been populations of crisps-lovers in exotic places, an increased global network of pot-holed roads and a more geographically widespread befuddlement about the síneadh fada.

Some nights while sitting on a bus in London he'd hear an Irish accent in the background and he'd think, that person is Irish. Definitely Donegal. Or he'd be on the Tube or queuing in a shop and he'd hear a soft Clare lilt or a heavy Meath brogue and a feeling of – shudder the thought – longing would come over him. This dismantling of his critical barriers scared him and he tried to avert it but the longer he was away the more he thought of home. Of course, the minute he got home he couldn't stop thinking about getting away again.

Why couldn't life be simple and why couldn't he just feel at home, when at home?

It was all his Dad's fault. Dead many years now but still an ever lingering presence.

Though having worked for the Irish Tourist board, Bórd Fáilte, most of his working life, Ger Bodkin instilled in his elder son a complete contempt for his country.

'Always eradicate mediocrity, son. Accept only the best,' Ger used to say as he would share with Roddy his latest fantasy plan to eliminate another Irish show business second-rater.

'I'll run him down in the Mirafiori outside Clarinbridge during the oyster festival. So many lunatics on the road this weather, people won't think anything strange about it.'

The time was late summer 1980 and Dad had Waterford-born showband singer and latter-day Las Vegas sensation Brendan Bowyer in his sights.

'Although then they'd re-release 'The Hucklebuck' and it would be number one all over again, and I would have to listen to it non-stop, ad nauseam, so one of the main reasons for committing the crime, not having to hear that bloody song ever again, would be nullified and I would be confronted with an even worse outcome. Obstacles. Life is all about obstacles.'

Brendan Bowyer was safe. For now.

Ger never went through with his plans. He probably wasn't really serious in the first place. It was all just talk.

But all through Roddy's childhood and adolescence, Ger would keep coming back to this same topic. The cringingly inferior quality of Irish popular culture. In the car. On the way to Mass. And especially in front of the television. Having only that one television channel, RTE One, until 1978, had seriously unhinged Ger Bodkin. He took it personally. Why was God punishing him? The God he spoke to on a regular basis. Why did he have to do without *Parkinson, Starsky & Hutch* and *The Two Ronnies* and be forced to watch a television channel which considered one of its broadcasting highlights of the year *The John Player Tops Of The Towns*?

While walking with Roddy opposite Salthill church the following spring Ger spotted a poster for another up-and-coming event. Singing superstar Joe Dolan was coming to town. To do a gig in Leisureland. This time, Ger affirmed, an act of extreme violence leading to the welcome demise of the intended victim would have to be perpetrated.

'God, the women go for awful strange-looking things in this country, don't they?' he said, referring to the Mullingar sex symbol and shaking his head.

'And don't get me started on flippin' Dickie Rock. *I'll* spit on you Dickie! With hydrochloric acid!'

Ger stood looking at the poster of Joe. Big lapels. Big grin. Big deal.

'He's nothing but a third-rate Demis Roussos. Without the beard. And kaftan. And you know what I think of Demis Roussos!'

Ger had it all worked out. Gun down Joe at the entrance opposite Salthill Park before the gig and make his getaway to Barna and hide out in Connemara for a few days. But he knew it was hopeless. Where would he get the gun?

'It's so difficult in this country to buy any sort of firearm. Sure Jesus tonight, in America you can go into a shop, buy a gun and shoot the celebrity you hate the most. Or *love* the most. But here. It's impossible.'

Joe too was safe. For now.

Ger had a secret hit-list of candidates – his 'Crap Shoot' as he'd refer to it – in a special red-covered notebook. Red for blood. Politicians and show business figures. He wanted to completely obliterate all the no-talent chancers that dominated Irish life in the 1980s. These people are nobodies, he'd say. But they're *our* nobodies, Agnes would reply. They are still nobodies, he'd insist. None of them would make it internationally. Simple nobodies. Agnes would look at him, then add brightly, Gay Byrne would have made it. Setting aside his fork, Ger would just stare at her. But she'd continue to rhapsodise about the Irish broadcasting legend. If he'd stayed abroad, in the 1960s, he'd have made it, she'd claim. Ger would put down his knife. Then in a low sinister voice, he'd mumble, what did I say about mentioning that man's name at the dinner table. I don't want to hear any more about that man. That bloody man! But Agnes was having none of it. Mother had a stubborn side and would ensure the debate continued. Well, I don't care what you say. I won't have you doing him down in this house. Then she would start the next sentence with the two words that would ensure Ger reached a volcanic level of apoplexy. *Uncle Gaybo* is undoubtedly the best chat show host in the whole world. Ger would push back his chair and shake his head in exasperation, Jesus tonight! Don't call him that name! For Jesus sake! Sure, you are a year older than him, woman!

There would be a long pause. Roddy's ill-at-ease ten-year old brother Ronan, rabbit-caught-in-headlight-eyes, would seek assurance from his apathetic parent-hating fourteen-year-old sibling. Roddy would just shrug his shoulders and look down on his near empty plate.

'Can I have another fish finger?'

Both parents would bark in unison '*May*!'

'*May* I have another fish finger?'

'No. There's none left in the pan,' Agnes would respond tersely.

But she was now riled and wanted to continue the robust exchange with her husband. She would search around for other names from the firmament of the Irish light entertainment industry. Maureen Potter then! she'd proclaim. She'd have made it. They all said that. She'd have made it. Topped any bill. Anywhere. The Glasgow Empire. The London Palladium. Carnegie Hall. She even made some Nazis laugh way back in the 1930s. Ger would have had enough. A fist would be thumped on the table and he'd let out a roar – let's just drop the topic alright? Can a man not have his dinner in peace! There would be a moment of silence. He would calm down, then finally pronounce – I'll just say one thing about Maureen Potter, she's no Flip Wilson!

In addition, Ger passed on a less than favourable opinion of his native city to his two sons and Galway's position in the world was also a constant bone of contention between himself and Agnes. She loved Galway and always defended it.

'I don't care what people say, it's one of the best places to live in the whole world. The Atlantic next to us. Connemara up the road. Beautiful scenery. And the people. Great people. We definitely punch above our weight.'

Ger would snigger. He'd start forensically examining the matter.

'Do we? And tell me this now, if we're so good at punching above our weight, what major city in France is Galway twinned with?'

Agnes would know what was coming. Ger would grin malevolently.

'Is it Lyon? No. Toulouse? No. Marseille? No. Bordeaux? No. Lille? No. Montpellier? No. Nantes? No. Strasbourg? No. Rennes? No. Le Havre? No. Grenoble? No.'

He'd pause and shake his head. And go on.

'Reims? No. St. Etienne? No. Nice? No. Metz? No. Brest? No.'

Agnes would scowl at him. Ger would start to take pleasure in his French pronunciation.

'Amiens? Non. Perpignan? Non. Clermont-Ferrand? Mais, non. Avignon? Malheureusement, non.'

Agnes would suffer in silence and sigh tensely. Ger would savour the moment as his punchline approached.

'The place in France that Galway City is twinned with is a place so obscure that those two sons of ours have never even heard about it in their Geography class!'

Agnes would protest. But the fight was quickly going out of her.

'That's not true. Roddy, Mr. Baxter mentions Lorient now and again in his Geography class, doesn't he?'

Roddy wouldn't want to take sides but Agnes had always told him to be truthful.

'Not really mammy. Sorry. Mr. Baxter has never ever mentioned Lorient once in Geography class.'

THE TOO MUCH STUFF BLUES

The house in Kinvara is quite cluttered. Agnes has a propensity to store items and the place is 'chock-a-blocked' with things. She's always been that way. One evening she is out playing bridge – or as Ambrose likes to call it 'middle class bingo' – with her friends, Ida and Virgie. Roddy goes into her bedroom. He has promised Agnes he'll defrost the fridge and is looking for the hair dryer. An old tip from Lorraine. To expedite defrosting – use a hair dryer! Roddy starts rooting in Agnes's cupboard. He comes across all sorts of things. Bars of chocolate. Tights. Some old jackets. He smirks. Looks like he just didn't have enough girlfriends over the last fifteen years. He roots some more. He spots some cheap things Agnes has bought because they were 'a good bargain'. Items she's put away until she decides what to do with them or who to give them to. She is a great one for the 'good bargain'. Or the 'free stuff'. Agnes loves the 'free stuff'. Collect enough bloody milk coupons, clutter the place with bloody milk coupons until they are coming out of your ears so you can get a coffee-maker that you'll never use and just store away in your cupboard. Or another thing she loves doing is cutting out recipes from magazines and sellotaping them into a big loose-leafed notebook, but does she ever use any of these new recipes? She does not! The worst cook ever, west of the Shannon. Roddy is convinced of it. He wouldn't mind but her sister, his Auntie Nuala, had been a good friend of Theodora Fitzgibbon and knew how to make all her recipes. But Agnes? Sadly, culinary inventiveness, along with singing in tune and parking a car, are not part of mother's skill set.

He finally finds the hair dryer. Underneath an old Jilly Cooper novel. Plugs it in. Doesn't work. This is what happens to household objects when a parent gets older. A thing stops working, it is set aside, or falls under a Jilly Cooper novel and it just doesn't get replaced. Defrosting will have to wait.

He returns the hair dryer to where it was and spots something in the corner of the cupboard. He pulls it out. A calendar from last year. 2012. Agnes must have just dumped it there in early January. A replica of the calendar Lorraine and himself owned, the freebie *Irish Times* one, containing the best of Martyn Turner's cartoons. The one Roddy wrote his Comedy Covenant on. The one he smudged his blood on. He reflects for a moment. Maybe the goals he has set himself to achieve by September 30th are too unrealistic. After all, it is now nearly mid-April. And the break-up with Lorraine hasn't been easy. How can a man be expected to write blisteringly funny shit-hot comedy material during all this emotional turmoil? Time for a slight reappraisal. He decides to make another solemn pledge. Aloud.

'By Monday, September 30th, 2013, I, Roddy Bodkin, will have launched my stand-up comedy career.'

He leaves it at that. The gigging regularly and assembling enough material for the one-man show at The Edinburgh Fringe will have to wait.

Small steps before large steps.

He wanders into the spare bedroom where he sleeps. This is just as cramped. A stock room with a mattress.

A lifetime's accumulation of stuff stored here. Bet you Lorraine is happy with all that extra space in her house in Whitestrand Avenue since he moved out. She'd been clever, purchased it way back in 2002. Head screwed on properly, Lorraine Heuston. Roddy sits on the bed and looks around.

There are a few books. Some, once considered

cool and essential for a young man's understanding of life, that he never got round to finishing (or even starting) like Kerouac's *On The Road*. Others, considered uncool and middlebrow, that he actually did read and enjoy. What's so wrong in liking David Lodge?

Many DVDs and some old videocassettes. Mainly stand-up comedy ones he's picked up over the years. The Good. Dylan Moran. The Bad. Bobcat Goldthwait. The... What The Fuck?! Jim Davidson. Plus all those music CDs. (Even Roddy has dispensed with nearly all of his old audio cassettes over the years apart from one or two 1950s rockabilly compilations and a Fletcher Henderson cassette he purchased in Loughrea in 1990.)

He picks up a new CD holder he recently purchased from Amazon. He ordered the ugliest-looking one online. His reasoning was this. Last year he had ordered a nice-looking shower curtain from Amazon. But when it arrived it was undoubtedly the ugliest shower curtain he had ever seen. Lorraine was not impressed. So he figured, if pretty stuff from Amazon was in reality ugly, conversely ugly stuff might, in some bizarre way, be pretty. But it didn't turn out that way. The new CD holder is as ugly as it looked online.

He must stop buying CDs. But every time he's in town he always finds himself killing time in Red Rock West and purchasing a CD he'll never listen to.

The following morning, after the deceptively time-consuming Kinvara to Galway City bus trip, Roddy enters the HMV music store on William Street. As a self-professed expert on authentic early-to-mid-twentieth-century Americana he is standing, as usual, next to the ever depleted Jazz and Blues section. Which is now, as in all music shops, positioned next to the classical music section. Because it is considered old stuff. Dead stuff. Evicted from the hard drive of the present. Pre-1960. It does not count. Michael Bublé – that diminishing marginal Sinatra, that plastic hunk plunderer of the Great American Songbook – is committing atrocities to Cole Porter's 'I've Got You Under My Skin' over the shop's sound system. Roddy is in actual physical pain. He thinks about going up to the staff member behind the counter. Please don't play Bublé, he wants to say. I know I'm no hipster, more an apprentice fuddy-duddy, and all the young people (especially young women) love Bublé, and other older people with no taste adore him, but he's no more than a Harry

Connick Jnr. for slow learners. And just because he is new doesn't mean he is *doing* anything new. Or better. Put on the real stuff. Please, I beg you. The good stuff. Put on Chet Baker. Put on Sammy Davis Jnr. Put on Ray Charles. Blossom Dearie. Lee Wiley. Dinah Washington. Michael Bublé is the aural equivalent of a sliced white pan.

But Roddy doesn't go up to the counter. He stays where he is, being slowly and excruciatingly tortured by a bland hero for a bland era. He looks at some CD box sets. Box sets? More like crate sets! Where do people store all this stuff? Apartments aren't getting any bigger. He looks at a special offer. Ten CDs of jazz maestro Duke Ellington for four euro. That's not a special offer. That's an insult. They are just throwing this stuff away. It's like a junk sale. What an affront to Duke Ellington. Impossible to read the track listings. No information on the recording dates. Shoddily packaged. And this is not just the fate for The Duke. The legacy of all the great jazz men and blues men has been besmirched by a bulk-buying Walmart ethos. Sure, many of these tracks have free copyright, but does that mean they should be dismissively devalued in this way?

Buying music just isn't the same any longer.

Obviously the internet has radically changed things. But the act of physically purchasing music has altered also. Nowadays, he buys one of these CD box sets, plays it a month later, and three of the CDs are faulty. And guess what? He doesn't care. Because there's so much of it anyway. Seven other CDs. At least a hundred other songs. Pummelled by excess. No. Must stop buying CDs. From now on. Definitely.

That night Roddy sits on the bed in the spare bedroom in the house in Kinvara. He has finally defrosted the fridge with that new hair dryer he purchased earlier. Agnes is snoring fitfully downstairs. He sighs and attempts to create space for two specially reduced Ben Webster CDs, a Red Norvo compilation, some obscure Memphis Minnie blues recordings from 1942 and that Duke Ellington whopper ten CD hamper.

ON THE STREET WHERE YOU LIVE

It is difficult to imagine the word 'erudite' and the words 'Ambrose Hegarty' in the same sentence but Roddy does acknowledge that his closest friend, though a rambling ranting social outcast much of the time, has a wide-ranging and very impressive general knowledge. None more so than in the area of culture. For years Ambrose has quoted this Greek guy, some poet, 'In those fields and streets where you grew up, there you will always live and there you will die.' Up until recently, Roddy never took the quote seriously, but since returning to Galway from London and living with Agnes in Kinvara, he has thought of the quote quite often, especially since he's begun having this recurring dream.

He is an adult. But he's dressed like an eight-year-old. He is wearing slightly ill-fitting yellow shorts and a stripy T-shirt, and is carrying an orange football under his arm.

The house where he grew up, and spent his first twenty-three years, was on Dalysfort Road in Salthill and his childhood friend Dermot O'Toole's house was at the bottom of this road. In his dream, he slowly walks down the road, past the houses of all the people he knew, to see if his friend, Dermot, is in and if he wants to come outside and play football. Roddy steps softly on cartoon cotton wool, almost floating in a dream-like manner (after all it is a dream) past all the houses. Past all the neighbours he knew long ago. Most probably dead now. Mrs. Mannion. Mr. and Mrs. Canavan. Mr. Butler. Mr. and Mrs. Lee. He sees Josie Foley from number thirty-eight. Snoopy Josie. Still alive. Looks ninety.

He then spots Mr. Quirke from number forty-four coming out the front door. Though stooping slightly he has aged well. Mr. Quirke takes in his bin. Some things are constant, Roddy muses, having a daydream within his dream. This is what men do. And will always do. They put out the bin and they take in the bin. All their lives. The seven stages of man and bin. Things may have gotten more complicated over the last few years. More than one bin. Different coloured bins. Different days on different weeks to put out the bin. And take in the bin. But despite all these difficulties, man will adapt. And survive. And keep putting out and taking in the bin.

Roddy passes more houses. Still that floaty feeling. Weightless feet. Almost gliding. Inches from the ground. He sees Mrs. Loftus sitting in the front room of number fifty-two. The front garden had been re-landscaped. Gravel now. A true sign of widowhood. Mr. Loftus must have died in the last eighteen months. The person who mows the lawn is dead. Get rid of the lawn.

He looks at the other side of the street. Peter O'Dea lived across the way at number fifty-seven. A year older than Roddy. He was Roddy's 'randomly chosen playmate who Roddy never liked'. A real-life memory infiltrates his dream. One summer Roddy was bored playing with his new toy truck. Agnes was becoming slightly exasperated with him as he was gradually entering a state of low-level whinging during his mid-afternoon torpor. Suddenly, she looked out the window and saw another bored child playing with his latest toy across the road. And then she came up with a great idea. 'Look it, Peter O'Dea is out there, on his own. Why don't you go out and play with Peter like a good fella.' Roddy replied precociously and cogently, 'Because I don't like Peter, mother. Just because he lives across the road and we're almost the same age, doesn't mean we get on with each other! Why do most adults think all children will get on with each other? How offensive! Do you get on with every adult? No. You intensely dislike Mrs. McNally of the parish committee. I've heard you complain about her on the phone. I don't ask you to have a cup of tea with Mrs. McNally, do I?'

The real-life memory bit ends just before he replies precociously and cogently.

Roddy finally reaches his dream destination. The O'Toole house. He opens the gate of number sixty-eight. And walks slowly up the driveway. A tiny dog approaches him – obviously not Benjy, who died tragically in 1981 after being run over by a Thermo King float in that year's St. Patrick's Day Parade – and starts yapping ferociously. Even in dreams, dogs never give him a break.

He rings the doorbell. There is no answer. He rings again. A white-haired lady tentatively opens the door. Mrs. O'Toole squints and though slightly confused when seeing, to her, a barely recognisable Roddy, her upbringing and general friendliness compel her to stand in the doorway.

'Hi Mrs. O'Toole. Is Dermot in?'

She looks at Roddy.

'Roddy? Roddy Bodkin?'

'Yeh.'

Roddy nods. There is a moment's pause. For many years Roddy has had this theory. You only truly become a grown-up when you address the parents of your childhood friends by their forenames. Guess he still hasn't really grown up. In his dream world. Or in the real world.

'So is he there, Mrs. O'Toole?'

Puzzled, she looks at the orange football. Then looks at Roddy. Then looks at the orange football. Roddy smiles at her.

'No, Roddy love. He's in Botswana. He's an engineer.'

'Oh.'

Mr. O'Toole, removing his reading glasses, suddenly appears. His wife looks up at him.

'Willie. You'll never guess who it is.'

Mr. O'Toole scrutinises the specimen that is Roddy Bodkin.

'It's Roddy. Ger and Agnes's Roddy. Remember Ger and Agnes? They moved to Kinvara. Roddy Bodkin. From number sixty. In the old days.'

'Howye Roddy.'

There is a lot to be read from that 'Howye Roddy'. It conveys the thought why, in your early forties, are you standing outside my front door with a football looking for my son who hasn't kicked one in nearly twenty-five years. But the tone also tries to hide that thought with the forced warmth that fathers of childhood friends always addressed you with.

'Willie, will we ask Roddy in?'

Mr. O'Toole, slightly alarmed, doesn't have a chance to respond.

'Roddy, do you want to come in?'

'No. It's OK. I was looking for Dermot. Just tell him I called.'

Roddy turns to go.

'I will. He always rings Sunday. Goodbye Roddy. Lovely seeing you again.'

Mr. O'Toole nods and closes the front door and ushers Mrs. O'Toole through the inner door.

A strong melancholy overwhelms his nocturnal reverie. Things were so much easier in the old days. When he rang that O'Toole doorbell and asked 'Is Dermot in?', of course Dermot would be in. Where else would he be? He was *eight*. Roddy didn't have to phone Dermot in advance. Text him wondering if he would be free at four-thirty. Or maybe sometime next week. Dermot was always there. The world was constant. And never in Roddy's mind back then did he think that there would come a time when people would no longer be there and this world would no longer exist.

He closes the O'Tooles' gate after him and sighs. Still dreaming, on a whim, he decides to call on the McMahons, to see if Ivor McMahon is in, at number seventy-two, instead. He walks a little further, opens a gate and walks up a driveway. He tries ringing a doorbell. The doorbell doesn't work. He then knocks on the door. No response. Starts to bang on the door. He keeps banging. More vigorously. Yells. Hello? Louder. Hello? Anybody in? Hello? The door opens abruptly and he is greeted by a giant Macnas puppet with an enormous head, who jumps out and belches a large ring of fire. Roddy screams loudly.

Suddenly, Agnes opens the spare bedroom door in the house in Kinvara, and enters.

'What are you screaming about? Time for you to get up, Roddy Bodkin, it is way after ten. Your father wouldn't have put up with this sort of messing! I don't know what I'll do with you, at all.'

THE FISHERMAN'S MUSEUM

It is two months after the whole London catastrophe. Roddy is back living in Galway City. He has moved away from Kinvara and Agnes and has rented a small dingy flat in Palmyra Avenue, just off Sea Road. He'd become happily stagnant in Kinvara. Lost in his endless brooding over bygone times. The hold of the old. The pull of the past. The past was like a lover. He'd go to bed with the past. He'd wake up with the past. He'd fight with the past. He'd make up with the past. What was it American writer William Faulkner wrote? The past isn't dead. It's not even the past. Or something like that. Although William Faulkner is dead. So if William Faulkner is dead and that's in the past, how can the past not be dead? Roddy was becoming confused.

Thankfully, forthright farmer scribbler poet Ambrose Hegarty snapped him out of his confusion, during a phone call one evening while Roddy was having a pint in his new local, a charming old world country hostelry, The Travellers Inn.

'What's wrong with you, Roddy? You can't stay living with Agnes. You need to move out.

Otherwise, a few years down the line you'll end up being the DC!'

'The what?'

'The DC. Designated Carer!'

'Christ, never thought of that! Jesus. You're right. Filial duty is all very well, but, eh, duty should only go so far, right? Fair's fair. Yes. Time to move out. And she is pushing on. Pissed earwigs and all.'

'Nonie's eyebrows were more like slugs on ecstasy, God be good to her.'

'Glad we're having this chat, Ambrose. I love my mother, but at some future point, I don't want to have to… and then have to… and afterwards always having to…'

'It's a lot of responsibility. And you're talking to a man that knows. One can have one's fill of filial duty.'

'Lorraine always claimed responsibility was never my strong suit.'

How right Lorraine was. Amazing what the prospect of coordinating and overseeing the elder care regime for a loved one does to a man. Suddenly he finds a reason to do something else. Roddy is now gainfully employed as a museum attendant. A relative, Catriona, knew someone, Adrienne, who knew someone, Tessie. He is happy to get the job – money is tight, savings are low – and also, more importantly, because he knows that not many people are aware of this small fisherman's museum in the Claddagh. It is the most under-publicized museum in Ireland and he sees this as an ideal arrangement. Maybe, he can get some joke writing done on the job.

He turns up most days at ten o'clock after Tessie, the curator, has opened the museum. He gets into his uniform, an old cinema usher's outfit Tessie has wangled from her uncle who worked in the Savoy on Eglington Street in the 1960s, saunters up to the second floor where most of the exhibits are and sits on a chair. He looks around and takes out a biro and small notebook from inside his shirt pocket. He wants no distraction as he contemplates and creates doodles with his biro on the pad. What strikes him as humorous? What's his 'take' on things? What sort of 'comedy voice' does he have?

However, there are always one or two *enthusiastic* tourists, disrupting his concentration, mainly Germans, but also Spaniards or Italians that seem so *interested* in the museum's exhibits – old fishing nets and tackle, some very old black and white photographs of very poor people showcasing a timeless grubby squalor of Galway City, bits of old rowing boats and intact currachs and some items of clothing like the white Aran jumpers immortalized by the Clancy Brothers.

If it is a young couple and Roddy wants to continue with his thoughts and random scribbling he devises a strategy. As the couple forensically scrutinize an exhibit, and try to decipher the smaller English translation underneath the larger gaelic description – Tessie is a committed gaeilgeoir, misguided óinseach – Roddy gets up from his chair and walks over to the young couple. He stands close to them, feigning over-vigilance. At first they giggle self-consciously, mutter something to each other, but eventually Roddy still standing behind them and encroaching gradually into their personal space makes them quite uncomfortable. They move onto another exhibit and Roddy follows. They become slightly offended, thinking he is suspecting them of possible theft – even if there is nothing much to steal – and, increasingly agitated and paranoid, they decide to leave.

One time recently Roddy had quite a shock. More than six people were in the museum *at the same time*. He found this particularly stressful. A modest touring photographic exhibition of a tanned smiling American man's visit to Galway in June 1963 was temporarily running in a small room upstairs. The man in the photographs waved a lot and had a definite charisma. Unfortunately, he could never fulfil his stated wish for a return visit after his untimely and tragic death the following November in Dallas.

But Scandinavians prove the most hardy and persistent visitors. They aren't bothered by Roddy encroaching into their personal space as they always seem so enthralled by the recreated Galway Hooker (the name of a fishing boat, Roddy had to explain once to a confused English tourist) in the corner of the museum.

Ambrose suggested a strategy.

'Onions and garlic are yer only man.'

'What?"

'A feed of onions and garlic. For tea every evening. And jays, the next day you'll be stinking. No one will want to stand near you. You'll be a prime specimen of olfactory repellent. You'll be able to do all the writing you want.'

Roddy thanked Ambrose for the suggestion but declined. An endless diet of onions and garlic would remind him of his chronic halitosis during his teenage years which had thankfully cleared by his early twenties.

Some mornings Roddy tires of his attempts to come up with constructive comedy ideas and feels very frustrated. Just to distract himself from his paltry comedy output and feelings of abject futility, when some museum visitors are in his proximity he decides to actually engage with them. In the process, some old habits resurface. This morning, a middle-aged Australian couple are examining an early-twentieth-century black and white photograph of some exhausted fishermen from the Aran Islands. Roddy gets up from his seat and approaches them.

'Look pretty tired don't they?'

The Australian couple nod at the friendly Irish museum guard.

'Those island fishermen are from the Aran Islands. Some islands off the coast of Galway. If you have the time you should go there. Amazing place. Anyway, those fishermen would have been exhausted from a day out trying to kill the Modh Coinníollach.'

The couple listen intently.

'Half Moby Dick. Half Loch Ness Monster. The Modh Coinníollach was a fearsome sea creature found off the west coast of Ireland during the late-nineteenth and early-twentieth centuries. It binged itself on every type of fish and marine life up and down the shore of Connacht and beyond, so obviously nothing remained for the fishermen to catch. So groups of under-employed fishermen, like our friends here in this black and white photograph, would take it upon themselves to go out on perilous expeditions to try and slay their colossal gluttonous foe. The actual size of the Modh Coinníollach was the subject of much debate. Some people said it was as big as a zeppelin, but other people claim the Modh Coinníollach had a more modest dimension and was just the size of a normal thatched cottage.'

The Australian couple are enthralled.

'Now I know what you're wondering. You're wondering, how come there's nothing about the Modh Coinníollach in any of the guide books. Well you see, when bad things happen in Ireland, we prefer to forget about it and never mention it again and on the morning of October 12th 1931, also known as Black Modh Coinníollach Day, a very bad thing happened. Just outside Clew Bay, up in Mayo. It was a bright fresh day, calm conditions, when fifty-three fit young men, Gaels to their core, set off in ten currachs, those wooden-framed

Irish boats like the one you see over there, to finally eliminate the Modh Coinníollach. But he was waiting for them. Quiet as a freakishly ginormous church mouse. But more importantly, he hadn't eaten for two hours. Those fifty-three fit young men didn't stand a chance.'

Roddy pauses for effect.

'They were never seen again.'

The couple look at Roddy, then at each other.

'But that's not all. The Modh Coinníollach subsequently suffered from indigestion, his repast did not agree with him, and he started to belch fiercely underwater. These belches were of such magnitude that, the following morning, they created the very first tsunami ever in Ireland, which caused extensive damage as far inland as Castlebar and Kiltimagh.'

The couple are dumbstruck. Roddy smiles. He's enjoying this.

'Anyway, enough about the Modh Coinníollach, I'll let the two of you get on with your visit to the museum and enjoy the rest of your time in Galway.'

A UNITED IRELAND

Roddy Bodkin has never been all that keen on striking up conversations with strangers in bars. But on this particular night he is going to do just that. What has caused this change of heart?

Murder most foul.

Every time somebody is murdered, and it is reported on the television news, the victim seems to be 'a quiet person who kept to themselves'. Statistically, Roddy thinks, just once, there must have been an ebullient, gregarious, chatty murder victim, in all those years. But no. In a lifetime of watching news on the television, a murder victim is always 'a quiet person who kept to themselves'. This has caused Roddy some anxiety for he too is a 'quiet person who keeps to himself'. And given the ever-increasing crime rate he seems an obvious candidate for a random homicide. Therefore, he has decided to change. To avoid being murdered he will force himself to talk to people and become more friendly with his fellow man.

He also welcomes any excuse to leave his new accommodation, that non-homely hovel in Palmyra Avenue.

Roddy enters PJ's, his local pub in Lower Salthill. He loves the unchanging decor. 1970s flash. He spots a free stool next to a grunting, middle-aged man who is holding a whiskey. He would have usually stood at the bar in circumstances like this or sat elsewhere, but new friendly frightened-of-being-murdered-in-his-flat-because-he-liked-to-keep-to-himself-Roddy decides he will sit next to the man. The man doesn't look Irish. A tourist. Not German though. Or French. The oversized white trainers give American Frank McGinty away. As Roddy approaches, Frank moves a stainless steel object on the counter. It looks like an urn. Roddy catches the barman Malachy's attention.

'Pint, Malachy.'

The barman places the pint in front of Roddy and Frank orders another whiskey.

Roddy stares at the urn. Frank drawls.

'My mom's cremains are in it. Her cremated remains. She was Irish. People's name was Ma-*hone*-y. From Oranmore. Just down the road. I'm Frank McGinty.'

'I'm Roddy. Hi. So, a returning yank scattering some ashes huh? '

Roddy takes a gulp. The small talk is going

well. Frank sighs.

'I wish it was that easy. She was an Irish republican. All her life. Uncompromising. Extreme. Her name was Nora. You could say she put the *Nora* in *Nora*id.'

Roddy, having only half-heard, is confused.

'What?'

'Remember Noraid? They used to send money to...'

'Oh yeh.'

Frank continues.

'You're not one yourself are you, buddy? A sympathizer of the armed struggle? I mean I don't want to discredit your beliefs...'

'No. No. I mean... not really. Twenty-six counties. Thirty-two counties. Does it really matter? The same sky. The same rain. The same insularity.'

Frank becomes reflective.

'She passed eleven months ago. And she stipulated in her will that she wanted her ashes to be brought home to *Ire*-land, and get this, to be scattered in all thirty-two counties.'

The next whiskey arrives. Roddy registers surprise.

'What? How *big* was she?'

'Big-boned. A farm girl. But not *that* big. I mean

the cancer shrunk her a lot at the end. And now I'm worried. I mean there was about two thousand five hundred grams in this urn. Thirty-two counties? That's about seventy-eight grams per county. I have to be very careful with my scooping. And she wants me to scatter an extra big scoop outside Stormont Castle. Up in the North of *Ire*-land. Just to, in her words, 'show those goddamn Unionist black proddy bastards'.'

Roddy sniggers into his pint.

'How much have you left?'

'Well, I don't know. *And* I'm running behind schedule. *And* I wouldn't want to run out of the stuff before her wish was fulfilled. Especially if I only got round to scattering in twenty-six counties. She'd never forgive me for that, buddy. Would start spinning in that urn.'

He looks wearily at the stainless steel flask on the counter and begins downing another whiskey.

'She was a devout Catholic, but she insisted on being cremated rather than going into the ground, because she felt one thing was more important than eternal salvation – Irish Freedom. And she thought that by scattering her ashes in the thirty-two counties, she would in death, in her own way, unify the country. Want another drink?'

'Yeh. Thanks.'

'Barman!'

Malachy the barman is busy collecting glasses. Frank turns to Roddy.

'What's the story around here? Do you get a free one after four drinks like in the States?'

Roddy laughs.

'*Here*? No way.'

Frank drums his fingers on a beer mat and moves his head towards Roddy.

'The thing is, with her first anniversary coming up I finally had to come over here. I gave myself a month to do all thirty-two counties because I've got to be back stateside by the first. I've been here ten days. I've only done Limerick, Cork, Clare and Galway. And so many things have gone wrong. Crashed my rental car. Busted my elbow. Picked up a lip infection on the Blarney Stone. Could be herpes. What do I know?'

Frank upturns his inner lip and faces Roddy. Roddy grimaces.

'Doesn't look great.'

'Spilled some of the ash on the carpet of my B&B outside Doolin. It's not really ash by the way, only light grey dried bone fragments.'

'Yeh, I read it's mainly just the femur at the end.

Femurs are very sturdy.'

'And now I've picked up this god awful cold with the weather. What is it with the climate here? One morning last week, outside Adare, I was putting on my raincoat, taking off my raincoat, putting on my sweater, taking off my sweater, putting on my sunglasses, taking off my sunglasses... It was exhausting! Four seasons in five minutes.'

Roddy offers support.

'The Irish weather can do your head in.'

Frank yawns wearily.

'I've been stuck here in Galway for the last two days. Maybe I'll just dump it somewhere and get a flight out of Shannon in the morning.'

'You can't do that. She's your mother.'

Frank begins to reflect. As he starts to speak he keeps staring at the blue bags of dry roasted peanuts, like a display of small rectangular rosettes that hang on the back wall of the bar.

'I tell you she was a tough old broad. Difficult. No saint. That's all I'm saying. You know what she used to call me? Disappointment Number Two. My older sister Loretta, was Disappointment Number One. But you're right. Now that I'm here I might as well finish things. But I need transport. A guide. Someone who knows the country. I got a list here. She wrote down some specific scattering places in her will. Places of famous IRA ambushes or uprisings. Or something.'

Frank roots in his jeans. A squashed list emerges. Frank unfolds it.

'Sheemore, Leitrim. Where's that? I got to go to Scramogue, County Roscommon. An ambush there in 1921. How the hell do I get there? Or Vinegar Hill? What's a Vinegar Hill?'

'It's to do with the rebellion of 1798. It's in Wexford. Near Enniscorthy.'

Frank continues down the list.

'Another crazy-sounding place. Soloheadbeg. In Tipperary.'

'Oh, that was the beginning of the whole War of Independence. That's very important historically. '

Frank's mood lightens.

'You know these places? Hey, have you got transport? I'll pay. I've got lots of dough. It's not a problem.'

Roddy sighs and shakes his head.

'Sorry. I don't own a car. My friend Ambrose does. But he's a lunatic driver. You wouldn't want him driving you around.'

Frank looks mournful.

'Oh. Too bad.'

The pub is filling up. Roddy spots forthright farmer scribbler poet Ambrose Hegarty, at the other side of the bar and decides to join him. He bids Frank farewell and wishes him luck on his travels.

Ambrose looks up as Roddy approaches him.

'Howye. Thought it was you. Who's yer man?'

'Just another visiting yank.'

'Listen, I want to talk to you. I have an idea.'

There is a pause.

'Roddy, why don't you set up your own comedy club? Here. PJ has a room upstairs. Move on from the London thing.'

'Me?'

'You could be your own MC. Never much pressure on the MC. It'll give you time to develop your act. You've never done a gig before. Right? You don't have any material. Right? I still think my 'fierce conundrum' stuff has great potential but if you want to pass on it, so be it. Anyway, so you've no experience. No material. So you'll be absolutely shite starting off. Right?'

'Thanks for the confidence boost.'

'No, no, listen, listen so here's the thing. If you get really bad acts to perform on the same bill as you, you'll start looking good. You'll be MC. You'll be introducing crap acts. You can build up your material between the acts. You'll look the best. Maybe call the evening The Truly Awful Comedy Club. Go for that auld irony sort of thing. That's all the rage nowadays.'

'Great idea, Ambrose! Perform with some really bad acts. Where would I find these acts?'

'Well, here's the thing. I bumped into Cormac Creedon in McSwiggan's last night, he's left the Isle of Man and moved to Galway permanently, said something about 'the wild free spirit of the people and the general arty vibe of the place' – fuckin' deluded eejit – anyway, that's where I got the idea. He was talking about all these acts he knew in the old days. He says he plans to run a sort of a therapy and holistic wellness weekend for failed comedians and entertainers once a month in the wilds of the Burren, in an old converted coach house near Ballyvaughan. He's going to call it The Bad Act Clinic. He is basically helping people in show business, who have been traumatised by the persistent negative reaction their acts received over the span of their careers, to come to terms with their past and move on. The first one will be on Saturday week.'

'But he already knows us. How do we get in?'

'Auld Ambrose is always working the angles!

I told him we were interested in getting involved in the wellness industry and asked could we come along and observe things. He said no problem.'

Roddy is incredulous.

'He believed you?'

'Roddy, we're dealing with an individual who believed that being a home-based anti-Irish comedian was a good idea.'

It is two hours later. Ambrose has already departed. Malachy barks 'Have ye no homes to go to?' in the background, as he picks up some empty glasses and attempts to clear the pub of the odd boozy straggler. Malachy has used this expression for years but Roddy finds it a little insensitive nowadays given the ongoing global homelessness crises.

Roddy goes to the gents. He notices a vacant cubicle at the back, as the urinals have already been annexed by a group of loud boisterous young lads and their splashing members. On entering the cubicle, he spots a stainless steel flask on the cistern. Poor Nora McGinty. A United Ireland will have to wait.

AGNES

Mother is mithered, Roddy would always say in moments like this and Agnes *was* bothered. Hassled. Anxious. No use denying it. Having to get the house ready for visitors. Having to 'put on a good show'. 'Not to let the side down.' What side? There was only herself in it now. She should have arranged to meet Alice and Geoff in Galway. In Eyre Square. In The Great Southern Hotel or Meyrick's or whatever they call it now. But a few months back, when first cousin Alice rang from Bristol, and said herself and Geoff would be over in late May, Agnes, without thinking, and thrilled to hear from Alice after all this time, invited them to stay for a night or two in the house in Kinvara. Not such a good idea, now.

She'll have to get that Molly woman in to do the cleaning. Virgie Hanrahan highly recommends her. But to be honest, Agnes isn't sure. It's such a pity Maura Lynam 'hung up her hoover'. Maura was great. Agnes got on like a house on fire with Maura. And Maura was punctual. Every Thursday morning for the last fifteen years Maura would turn up at ten o'clock on the dot. At first Agnes felt strange letting someone in to do the cleaning, but after Ger, the Lord have mercy on him, got sick and all that, and then afterwards all her niggly health problems started kicking in, sure she wasn't able for it anymore and she didn't mind. She even stopped 'monitoring' the work after a few weeks. No point getting bothered if the cleaning woman doesn't reach your standards.

Anyway, what Maura lacked in thoroughness she made up for in personality. The lads didn't take to her as much, though. There was that debate about the missing nail scissors in early 2007 when Ronan inferred Maura was a bit of a kleptomaniac, and one or two of her lipsticks did seem to mysteriously disappear over the years but this was a price to pay, Agnes believed, for the company and the craic. Maura was great craic. Some of those stories she came out with! A natural storyteller. The one Maura tells about that escaped llama from Fossett's Circus that ended up in her back garden still has her in stitches.

But then about six months ago, she noticed Maura was getting old. Maura started wheezing going up and down the stairs with the hoover. 'The old ticker,' Maura would say. She'd take more time at her tea break, cherishing the sit down and the chat. They'd compare all their ailments and pains. Their organ recital, Maura would joke. That's a good one, Agnes would say. Maeve Binchy came up with it, Maura would admit. I always preferred Jilly Cooper, Agnes would announce. Then they'd enjoy their silence, look out the window and slowly finish their tea.

Agnes misses Maura. This Molly one is younger, much younger. Always checking her bloody phone. She was introduced to her in Virgie's house the other day. Sure, how can you get any bit of work done if you're always checking your phone? Oh no, she's not that gone on that Molly one at all, at all.

Still the place will need to be cleaned for Alice and Geoff. She'd ring Ronan and ask if Jenny could help out but she'd be imposing a bit, and anyway herself and Jenny don't always see eye to eye. She always preferred Lorraine but Lorraine and Roddy have finally called it a day and a not totally unexpected development either, to be honest. A pity though. Roddy is coming out to visit tomorrow. She hasn't seen him since he moved back into town. She could rope him in to do some cleaning and housework. He owes her after she allowed him to leave all those flippin' CDs, DVDs and books and what have you in the spare bedroom. Arey, who is she fooling? He'll only make the place worse. She remembers years ago the only wall she'd allow him to paint in the house was that small back wall, behind all the pots and pans, under the sink in the kitchen. That fella is a DIY bull in a china shop.

Suppose, she'll have to get that Molly woman out, after all. That'll be the cleaning side taken care of.

But what about food? Now, she was never a great cook, Roddy and Ger, the Lord have mercy on him, never let her forget it, so what'll Alice and Geoff eat? Takeaways? No, we can't be having that. Roddy says that newly opened Indian takeaway isn't bad but she's never gone in for that sort of exotic stuff with her auld reflux oesophagitis and the auld helicopter pylori or helicobactor pylori, or whatever they call it, anyway her guests would expect something a bit better than that. Looks like it'll be The Seaview Bar and Restaurant for the both nights. Not cheap, and that meringue didn't agree with her the last time she was there for her seventy-fifth birthday a few years back but sure what can you do? Although she does remember Alice saying once that Geoff doesn't really go for seafood and

The Seaview Bar and Restaurant specialises in crab and prawns and oysters and what have you, so that could be another problem. Problems, problems, problems. Why can't she just calm down and 'play it by ear' as they say, but sure with the state of her hearing nowadays, what good is that expression?

BAD ACT CLINIC

'This is not about judgement. This is not about self-recrimination. This is not about punishment. This is about self-acceptance. I'll get the ball rolling on the first Bad Act Clinic gathering by telling you my story. All my life I wanted to be a great comedian. And when I was young I read somewhere that in order to be a great comedian you had to be depressed. Truly depressed. Look at W.C. Fields. Look at Buster Keaton. Look at Peter Sellers. Look at Phil Silvers. All my heroes. All big time depressives.'

The participants sitting around the 'Circle of Circumspection' in that chilly coach house near Ballyvaughan listen intently to Cormac Creedon.

'Anyway, so somewhere along the way I came to believe that being constantly depressed was a good career move. I worked on my depression. It was like a little flower. I watered it and nurtured it and gradually it grew and grew and I became the most depressed young man in North West Cork. I was thrilled with the progression of my depression. I would go to parties in the university and an attractive young woman would come up to me and pester me and say 'fancy a shift?' and I would reply, 'Please go away. I don't want any distractions. I can't afford to be happy. I want to let my melancholia breathe. I want to be consumed with despair. I want to achieve a complete sense of moroseness and spiritual isolation. This will improve my art and help me fulfil my life's ambition to become a great comedian.' But all this time, I was neglecting my comedy. I was becoming very miserable but I wasn't becoming very funny. I would do the odd gig. Developed an act. Became Ireland's only home-based anti-Irish comedian. In my head I decided I was going to be great. But soon I realized, I don't get to decide. Comedy is all about the audience being judge and jury. And after a few years it dawned on me that I'd never move beyond a certain level. Because the audience *had* decided. I was just an average act. Maybe even a bad act. I'd see other comedians getting bigger laughs than me. And they seemed like quite happy individuals. This troubled me. And I found it quite baffling. 'So they are happy and they are funny and I am unhappy and I am less funny. There must be some mistake. All those years of meticulous suffering, surely, could not have been a waste of time?' In a way it was a waste of time and after fifteen years of acute self-loathing, periods of unfettered substance abuse and regrets too many to mention, I decided enough was enough. I had to accept myself the way I was and the way things had turned out and I had to start loving myself again. And I'm still very much in the learning to love myself stage and I consider this Bad Act Clinic very much part of my journey also. I'd like you all now to get up from the 'Circle of Circumspection', repeat in unison 'comedy is no laughing matter' and give me a big group hug.'

Roddy looks at Ambrose. All the clinic participants stand up and embrace Cormac. Like Irishmen embrace. With extreme caution.

There is a lull as people take their places again.

'I think it is time now to open it up to the floor and hear some of your stories,' Cormac announces.

There is a long pause. Then a large man in a beard tentatively stands up at the back.

'My name is Eugene Thornton, and to my eternal shame, and something I can never forgive myself for, back in the politically incorrect days of the early 1980s, I did a Pakistani character who liked to tipple called Mustafa Drink.'

Ambrose looks down on his partially hidden

notebook and whispers.

'Jays, we have to get this fella for The Truly Awful Comedy Club.'

Eugene continues. 'I didn't know any better. I'm sorry. It wasn't my fault. When we were young we were fed a TV diet of highly offensive ethnic stereotypes. That stuff was considered funny in those days.'

Roddy nods at Ambrose and whispers.

'Lucky him. Must have grown up on the east coast with ITV, BBC One, and BBC Two.'

Eugene stands motionless. Forlorn and silent. Cormac approaches him. And motions to the others.

'What do you think fellas, time for another 'comedy is no laughing matter' group hug?'

Later in the proceedings. In low voices Roddy and Ambrose discuss possible first night acts for The Truly Awful Comedy Club.

They definitely want Eugene Thornton. On the scale of awfulness Dinny Bruce is a definite contender too. Dinny Bruce. Ireland's one time answer to Lenny Bruce, as he told the group. Dinny used to dress up as a farmer in big wellingtons and do these very long monologues in a west Kerry accent about the 'pigs' being always after him but he did confess that most audiences couldn't make out what in God's name he was talking about. The juxtaposition of that whole beat culture Greenwich Village world of the 1960s and the day-to-day drudgery of life in Sneem didn't really work.

They are also eager to book Presto Mulligan. Presto did a comedy magic act back in the 1980s. He was a poor man's Tommy Cooper. A very poor man's Tommy Cooper. A pauper's Tommy Cooper. Anytime he performed a trick that went wrong, he'd shout 'Hey Me!'

If Roddy and Ambrose were really stuck, they decide they'd also ask impersonator Colman Hall – 'he does them all'. Colman isn't even a 'ballpark impressionist', more a case of a 'nothing like it at all' impressionist. When he does a random impression and asks those in the room to guess who he is doing, everyone seems completely flummoxed. Roddy eventually guesses a name.

'Christopher Walken?'

Colman reacts in the negative.

Ambrose wonders aloud, 'Daniel O'Donnell?'

Colman shakes his head.

'Vladimir Putin?' Cormac suggests with slight desperation.

Colman sighs in disappointment and reveals all.

'No. It's my Miriam O'Callaghan.'

Ambrose looks down on the names on the list and mutters to Roddy.

'We're in the pink. It's a truly atrocious line-up for the inaugural evening of The Truly Awful Comedy Club. You'll be brilliant in comparison with any of these losers. However, I think we need just one more act to make it a show.'

Suddenly an excitable short man stands up.

'My name is Billy O'Brien. My grandfather was Charlie Cheese. Back in England in the late 1940s he did a double act with a fella called Chester Crackers. Cheese and Crackers, they were known as. They played the music hall circuit. Variety. Seaside resorts. You probably never heard of them. Long forgotten nowadays. Actually, there was enormous difficulty even recalling them in their own day.'

Billy continues.

'Anyways, to cut a long story short, what I'm trying to say is, I suppose that performing is in my blood and about twenty years ago I also did an act. I was a ventriloquist. A slightly unorthodox ventriloquist. But I didn't care. I was full of energy. I was young. I just wanted to get up there. I'd come onstage in nothing but my underpants. And I would commence to converse with my genitals. I was known as Billy and His Talking Testicles.'

Ambrose clenches his fist. He looks at Roddy and mutters.

'Jesus, we have a line-up. The first night of The Truly Awful Comedy Club looks like it's all booked up!'

DATE FOR RODDY BODKIN

Some years ago, American film actor Nick Nolte was arrested by the California Highway Patrol while driving erratically in Malibu. He was charged with one count of driving under the influence of alcohol and one charge of driving under the influence of a controlled substance. His mugshot was taken while in police custody and it featured prominently in the following morning's news.

His hair is long and askew. Blow-dried by a benign nuclear bomb. He stares intensely at the camera with a slight sadness in his eyes and looks bats-in-the-belfry insane.

Most mornings, after waking from a deep slumber in his flat in Palmyra Avenue and looking at himself in the bathroom mirror – a fright for sore eyes – Roddy thought of that mugshot. But by mid-morning as he strolled into work at the Fisherman's Museum, his resemblance to Omaha, Nebraska's fourth most famous actor – after Marlon Brando, Fred Astaire and Montgomery Clift – had receded somewhat.

Still, as he fiddled with his biro and small notebook in the museum, still more doodling than actual coherent sentences leading to jokes, he felt like he was in the throes of a full on mid-life slump. Time to turn a corner. If only he could find where the corner was. He'd become so mired in his thoughts he recently passed a homeless man holding a placard saying 'Change, Please' and said to him 'Yes. I must. Thank you for the advice.'

He met Fiona Sheehy while smoking a cigarette outside Freeney's pub on High Street. He'd only taken up smoking, at the age of forty-three, as a chance to meet some women. He had to start getting out there again after the whole Lorraine debacle. And to lose weight. Twenty years ago he had fire in his belly. Granted, a small fire. More like a campfire. Now all he has is the belly. They say that inside every fat man is a thin man trying to get out. Or as someone once said, an even fatter man trying to get in. But Roddy knew his substantive tissue had become a substantive issue.

He *had* thought he might get lung cancer from the taking-up-smoking decision. But looking on the positive side, if he lost weight it would decrease his chances of getting bowel cancer.

Joining a gym would be healthier. But then he would be confused with a person whose earning power was in that cherished ABC demographic rather than slightly above the average industrial wage in Burkina Faso. (While on that topic, given Roddy's modest earnings he was sticking to Drum tobacco and rizlas.) And gyms imply exertion. And there was the small matter of male pubic hair on display. Roddy always became squeamish when exposed to male pubic hair. And then there would be the questions. The prying questions. The tyranny of eternal male competitiveness.

'What do *you* do, Roddy?'

Roddy hates being asked that question. A job gives you a sense of identity. He doesn't have that sense of identity. Not since working at Fleming Travel all those years ago. All the other jobs, since, were transitory in nature. And now another temporary posting in The Fisherman's Museum. Maybe he should start saying he is a comedian.

Fiona flicks away some ash and looks at him.

'And, what do *you* do Roddy?'

Roddy pauses for a moment. The words 'I'm a comedian' just can't come out of his mouth. He'd feel strange saying it. Also, it may lead to complications. She might say, never seen your act, where do you play? She might ask what kind of stuff you do? She might say she hates comedians. A lot of women hate comedians. Then again, she might say, I love comedians. A lot of women love comedians.

Eventually he says the next thing that pops into his head.

'I'm a stalker of my dreams.'

What a cool thing to say. Must be the cigarettes talking.

Fiona smiles. A mysterious man. Or a complete chancer. Still, not bad looking.

'What sort of dreams?'

Roddy is feeling confident.

'Dreams that scream lift-off.'

Fiona giggles.

'Can I get on board?"

'Sure thing.'

After some more flirting, a cinema date is arranged for the following week.

Six days later Roddy waits for Fiona outside the Omniplex on Headford Road. There is definitely an attraction. This could lead places. They had agreed to see a new Ben Stiller comedy. Roddy is slightly anxious but inhales from his cigarette. This calms him. What a wonderful sensation. He should have started smoking years ago. There is something about the aura of a smoker. When a man sits on a bench and stares into space, he is just a man. But when a man sits on a bench, stares into space while smoking a cigarette, he's something completely different. He's a philosopher. A man with a past. A man with a future. He is more than just a man. He's an *interesting* man. It is true. Smoking is cool and Roddy wants to be like them all. Bogart. Belmondo. Beatty.

Warren, obviously. Not Ned.

A half hour has passed. Still no sign of Fiona. He is standing at the back of the queue inside the crowded Omniplex.

Roddy looks around and becomes preoccupied as he notices an extremely noisy group of young people ahead of him. About ten of them. Boys and girls. Apprentice gurriers and gurrierettes. He senses trouble.

Tension grips him. He wonders what movie the group are planning to see.

He has no problem with gurriers and gurrierettes going to the cinema.

They have every right to go to a movie in the cinema. Just not the movie he is going to. With his date. He doesn't want to be annoyed by laughter in the wrong places or comments out of context. Or the prospect of laughter in the wrong places and comments out of context. A night of all round boisterous yobbery could be in the pipeline. They'll be getting up every ten minutes, giggling and going out the exit door. Then when the first three get back after much disruption and retaking-their-seats-inconvenience, another two will get up to go out. And this will go on for two hours. And the trouble is no one will complain. Nobody complains nowadays. Because, there's no point. There's no one to complain to. Ushers became extinct sometime late last century. The rest of the cinemagoers will just have to 'suck it up'. And if it isn't trainee yobs creating havoc it's the popcorn munchers munching from their large seaworthy vessels of popcorn. Or the device-dependent low-attention-span millennials, scrolling their Facebook page when they get bored, to see if Shona and Conor are having a fun time scuba diving in Malta.

He looks at his watch. Still no sign of Fiona. It was a casual arrangement anyway. Mobile numbers hadn't been exchanged. She said she'd lost hers and had to get a new one.

His anxiety is mounting. Goes out and has another smoke.

Why does he get so perturbed in situations like this? He doesn't want Fiona to see him this way.

At such an early stage. Give the relationship a few months, at least, before she is exposed to Dr. Jekyll and Mr. Curmudgeon. Close blood relative of Mr. Routine. Mr. Curmudgeon. Easily irritated by the foibles of humanity. Especially noisy foibles. Noisy young foibles.

Back inside. Fiona still hasn't arrived. Roddy starts thinking about Lorraine. The sudden end that had been coming for a while. All the things that went wrong. Could they have been fixed in time? If only he had changed a little bit. Met her halfway. And hadn't bought that cursed Dark Chocolate Surprise Valentine's Heart! Should have tried more with Lorraine. Took her for granted. He let her get away. Is he crazy? He'll never find anyone like Lorraine again. And now he's got to stay mentally positive with possibly somebody new. Starting tonight. On this date. Maybe he's not ready. His mood has turned. He hates those shrieking youngsters. The caterwauling of the girls in harmony with the voice-having-just-broken gruffness of the boys. Not a care in the world. All attitude and zits. Hormones exploding. Him and the rest of the queuing public the collateral damage.

Finally, an anonymous recorded voice tells the youngsters to go to cashier number seven. They go over to the ticket seller. They giggle and fuss and josh and buy the tickets. Which movie? Roddy strains to hear. He then scrutinizes the big display screen. With all the film listings. Twelve cinemas. Two movies are starting at nine o' clock. The Ben Stiller comedy in cinema four. And the latest movie with Steven Seagal in cinema ten.

Which movie would a bunch of high-spirited, very irritating, spotty teenagers want to see?

If Fiona turns up now they will have to take their chances.

Flee.

A voice whispers from the back of his head. A familiar voice.

Go. This evening isn't working out. Too stressful. Too many variables. I predicted this.

Mr. Routine is right. He *had* predicted this. Many times, over the last week.

Just leave. If you go now, you'll be home just in time to start scoffing at Tubridy on RTE One.

Yes. Scoffing at Tubridy. One of Roddy's favourite hobbies. Leave this all behind. The never-ending wait for Fiona. The potential problem with maddening group noise in the cinema. Just get the hell out. Thanks Mr. Routine. Once more you've brought a calm appraisal to proceedings.

Roddy purposefully walks out of the lobby and hurriedly crosses the road. As he picks up pace in the falling rain he notices Fiona smiling and chatting to a taxi driver as she gets out of a taxi. He strides straight ahead and doesn't look back.

THAT LOVELY DUTCH COUPLE

Summer in Galway.

Four words.

Pan-de-fucking-monium.

In July, after the cultural entrées of the Film Fleadh and the Arts Festival, comes the main dish – the Galway Races at Ballybrit – that six-day jamboree of horses, drink and vomit, primarily populated by the spray tan and helicopter-renting set. Ireland's version of gaudy Eurotrash.

To sum up, a month of relentless liver damage with a soupçon of culture and sport thrown in.

In recent years, Roddy rarely went out during this time of year. This summer, however, he would have been compelled to venture out, to his workplace in the Fisherman's Museum, but in an example of idiotically comical bad timing, Tessie had decided to close the museum in early July for renovations thus missing the potential windfall of the tourist season. Roddy is privately relieved. He was incapable of writing any comedy material in the museum environment and is hoping a few hours sitting at his kitchen table every morning with his laptop may prove more productive.

When this doesn't prove more productive and comedy inspiration seems as elusive as Lord Lucan riding Shergar through The Bermuda Triangle he leaves his flat to go for a walk and is unfortunately confronted, everywhere, by a throng.

He has to continually sidestep one of the multitude of tourists taking photographs. Or wait for them to take a photograph. Why should he have to stop his journey to wait patiently for a tourist to take a photograph? And what is there to photograph in Galway City, apart from the medieval gem that is St. Nicholas' Church? The one place he treated with reverence during his time working for Historical Walking Tours Galway.

Lynch's Castle? Not much of a castle. Sort of a greyish building housing some ATM machines inside.

The Spanish Arch? An old small archway of extremely modest historical significance. What really galls him is Spaniards taking a photograph of the Spanish Arch. *Not exactly the aqueduct in Segovia!* OK, he's never actually been to Segovia, but he'd seen a picture of it once in a coffee-table book about Castilian Spain that his mother received as a Christmas present in 1982.

One afternoon he becomes intrigued by the amount of tourists who still take photographs using digital cameras instead of smartphones. He is walking hurriedly across the Salmon Weir Bridge when he sees two tall, blond, knee-length-shorts-wearing visitors. Nordic. Possibly German. They have taken some photos of the fast-flowing river Corrib and of one another and suddenly start to look around for a potential photographer to take a photo of the two of them. Roddy is no Annie Liebovitz but sadly there is no one else on the bridge. He is trapped.

Jürgen – he looks like a Jürgen – approaches him.

'Excuse me please. Could you take our photo?'

Roddy sighs. He is handed a camera the size of a teabag.

'You just have to press this button.'

Roddy peers through the tiny viewfinder and tries to get the healthy, tanned, North European couple in shot. Such tall people for such a small camera. They beam. Roddy finally clicks. Jürgen comes over.

'Thank you.'

Roddy nods and goes on his way. While waiting at the traffic lights he observes Jürgen checking the picture.

People can do that nowadays, Roddy reflects. They don't have to wait until Wednesday next week because of a long weekend to get the photos developed. They can check it right away. People live in an instant world. No waiting. But do people still gain time? Maybe not. Lots of things are instant nowadays but people lose what they gain with other stuff that takes longer. Queuing for train tickets. Takes much longer now because everyone pays by credit card. The train journeys might be quicker but the queuing takes longer. Whatever is gained somewhere gets lost elsewhere.

Roddy's (in his view) profound meditation on modernity and the concept of time is suddenly interrupted when he notices Jürgen delete the photo that he, Roddy, had just taken. Jürgen approaches another person, this time a female passerby, to take *another* photo!

Being extremely thin-skinned and painfully sensitive to any criticism, Roddy is livid. The female passerby smiles at the couple. She asks where the couple want to stand – *oh a perfectionist!* – and what background they want – *cannot stand perfectionists* – maybe the lighting would be better on this side of the bridge – *I can't believe this* – and then she takes the photo. She immediately offers to take another. Just in case. She takes a second one. She hands the camera back and nods at the couple. They nod back, smiling. With an obvious interest in photography – *she probably takes photography classes every other night of the week, looks like a type that does loads of those self-improvement evening classes* – the female passerby waits as Jürgen, who doesn't seem to mind, checks the two photos. He is happy. So is his partner. The female passerby has a quick look. She is not completely satisfied with her work – *for fuck sake, this takes the biscuit* – and she suggests she take one more. Jürgen and his partner, slightly uncomfortable, agree. She positions the couple in the most optimum location available and snaps another photo. She knows instinctively this one is good. She hands back the camera, and waits a moment for Jürgen to upload the photo, and nod affirmatively. Yes. That is the one. No question. Everyone is extremely happy at the outcome as the female passerby bashfully waves goodbye and walks towards Galway Cathedral. Jürgen checks the last photo again. This is truly an excellent photo. In fact, they might get this one printed up, framed and put on their mantelpiece. They exhale after all that excitement, and walk towards the Town Hall

Theatre.

They spot a familiar face waiting for them at the traffic lights.

'So *she* took a nice photo, did she? Yeh?'

Awkwardness delays Jürgen's response. Roddy stares at him.

'More than one. Three. She took three. They were *all* probably better than mine. Yeh? Mine wasn't very good, no. No, you deleted mine. Immediately. Delete. Gone forever. Do you know what that does to my self-esteem?'

Jürgen looks at his partner. She looks at him and down at Roddy. Despite being a half-foot taller than Roddy she has slight trepidation in her eyes.

Roddy reloads. Both barrels.

'Do you know how offensive that was? At least you could have waited until I'd walked down the street and was out of view, but no, you had to check immediately, you... you... What are you, Danes?'

Jürgen finally speaks.

'Dutch. We are sorry. Our behaviour was unforgivable. Let us buy you a drink.'

Ten hours later, drunk and very naked, Roddy ponders on how a slight altercation on the Salmon Weir Bridge – his fault – had resulted in him lying in bed with a nude Dutch couple – their fault. Norbert Van Bruggen and Martita Berendsen have an interesting background. Norbert was a famous star of adult films in Europe during the 1980s who went by the moniker Ruud Bonk. Martita was involved in an authoritarian Dutch Reformist religious sect but left the sect in the late 1990s. On her first night of freedom, to see what bad things she'd been missing all those years (shades of Ger in that confession box), she decided to get drunk and rent a porn DVD. Which happened to star Ruud Bonk. It was love at first sight. She made it her new mission in life to track him down. Which wasn't difficult. Since leaving the porn industry he'd fallen on hard times and was literally round the corner from her recently acquired flat in Utrecht, trying out his new ill-advised busking career. She recognised him the next day, listened to him crucify the old Dutch carnival song 'Bloemetjesgordijn' and since that time they have been inseparable. They do everything together. Apart from one thing. Where they get one other person to join in. They look at Roddy.

'I'm Irish. We don't really go in for this sort of carry on.'

Norbert smiles. Martita smiles. She caresses

Roddy's left nipple. Roddy's embarrassingly large left breast musters a reaction. Roddy decides to keep talking.

'Ireland and Holland. We have lots in common. World Cup games over the years. Italy 1990. USA 1994. Euro Championship play-off late 1995.'

Norbert and Martita look at Roddy blankly. Not soccer fans. Roddy continues.

'That Dutch fella was kidnapped here in 1975, Dr. Tiede Herrema, by the IRA, do you remember him?'

Norbert starts softly sucking on Roddy's big toe.

'Ah now, cut that out Norbert. I'm not into that kind of messing.'

Roddy pulls away his foot and tries to get off the bed. But everywhere Roddy turns he still finds himself *on* the bed. A vast tundra of ruffled sheets.

'We always book a king-size', Martita whispers. 'We don't like three to be a crowd.'

'A king-sized bed? This is a floor-sized bed,' Roddy replies frantically.

Norbert breaks out laughing and starts to approach Roddy on all fours, purring like a Cheshire cat. Roddy edges backwards and resumes his overview of Hiberno-Dutch links.

'There was this other fella, over here, Gerritt van Gelderen, made wildlife programmes...'

'Wildlife. We've never tried it with wildlife,' utters a smirking Martita.

'Mother of divine sanctification!' Roddy yells. He starts jabbering.

'Of course, there's that tax arrangement U2 uses in the Netherlands. The Double Irish with a Dutch Sandwich. '

They look at him and laugh uproariously.

'Love the sound of that. We could try that here,' Norbert squeals.

Roddy shakes his head and mumbles.

'I walked into that one.'

Suddenly Martita moves towards Roddy's left side. Norbert crawls towards his right side. A sweaty fleshy pincer movement. Roddy is running out of things to talk about. Pincer movement! Bismarck! Idea!

'You two will love this. Otto Von Bismarck, that nineteenth-century German fella, said one time, if the Dutch lived in Ireland they'd feed Europe, if the Irish lived in Holland they'd drown!'

At this stage, Roddy feels like *he* is drowning. Under a sea of bodies – well, just the two. Inspired thinking is called for.

'I think I'm going to be *sick*!'

Norbert and Martita roll over and, hand on mouth, Roddy finally finds the edge of the bed and rushes to the bathroom. He spends two hours in the bathroom and realises how uncomfortable it is to be *fake* vomiting while trying to sober up.

Eventually, Roddy feels it is safe to unlock the bathroom door and that the passion in the room has subsided. He opens the door and slowly comes out. And furtively tries to find his clothes and his yellow and blue Krusty the Clown socks – *why did I have to put those on this morning*? Norbert looks up from the bed.

'Oh well. It wasn't to be.'

Martita giggles.

'Still. It was fun. And it's lovely to meet new people.'

As he makes his way out of the hotel Roddy vows to get out of Galway the following July. Maybe it is finally time to check out that aqueduct in Segovia.

MANBAGS AND RUCKSACKS

The prolonged nude interlude with Norbert and Martita had an unforeseen consequence. During the long blurry mayhem of that afternoon and evening Roddy had misplaced his call-and-text-only Nokia mobile phone. So finally, and reluctantly, he had to buy a smartphone. For years he had refused. Was bored when acquaintances showed him photos on their latest Android or iPhone. How presumptuous! I'm not *that* interested. One or two, maybe. But *thirty*! As a form of protest and as a way of making a point, he started carrying a small photo album in his rucksack so when someone showed him photos on their smartphone, he'd say 'They were lovely. Can I bore you now with a few of my photographs?' He'd remove the small photo album from his rucksack and start showing the person some random snapshots from his life. And then some more snapshots. And finally, one or two more. Nothing very recent though, which in a way was worrying. Lorraine was the photographer in their relationship. No one had taken a photograph of Roddy Bodkin for nearly a year. It was as if he no longer existed.

Having purchased a new smartphone he decided to embrace modernity further and finally dispose of his rucksack. Roddy's evolutionary journey in the 'what do I carry things in' area mirrored that of most Irish men of his vintage. In his late teenage years and well into his twenties Roddy was a proud bulky anorak man. Bulky anorak man was very common in Ireland from 1960 to 1990. He stuffed all sorts of things in his many anorak pockets like newspapers, apples, old pairs of gloves and portable bicycle lamps. One or two of this near extinct breed of bulky anorak man can still be spotted in the odd bookie's office.

But then anoraks became extremely 'uncool'. Suddenly, if you wore one, you were immediately suspected of being a child molester or someone who likes exposing himself on train station platforms. Roddy found this change in attitude and fashion very difficult to accept. He came from a part of the country where it rained fifty-two weeks of the year. Everyone wore anoraks. He was one of a tribe. The anorak people. Roddy always felt ill-at-ease with the concept of 'cool'. Maybe because he was never cool – Lodge over Kerouac, any time! Nik Kershaw over Nick Cave every time! And it never bothered him, apart from that slight infatuation recently with smoking cigarettes, because he realised many years ago that cool dates but uncool is timeless.

When anoraks became unfashionable, years of custom and tradition went out the window. A person had to leave that anorak at home and just wear a jacket. But jackets had much smaller pockets. And the anorak people found the sartorial adjustment difficult. And each time they went out, they'd catch heavy colds, influenza, sometimes even pneumonia. In order to survive they stayed indoors. Their social lives became non-existent. Instead, they would read about all sorts of things. The name of the bravery medal awarded to messenger pigeons during the Second World War. The DNA of a human being is 58% the genetic make-up of a cabbage. The fusiform gyrus is that part of the brain that specializes in processing faces or the fact that Stan Laurel's younger brother Teddy died of an accidental overdose of laughing gas on a dentist's chair in Los Angeles in December 1933. And then, on the few occasions they did go out, they would bore their friends with this newly found knowledge. Hence, their friends started referring to them as 'anoraks'. And, in an instant, the anorak-wearing 'anorak' became a kind of social leper.

Roddy would reluctantly have to make a compromise.

This compromise was the rucksack. Rucksacks became *de rigueur* about 1993. Overnight, the bulky anorak man became the rucksack man. At first, Roddy loved being a rucksack man. So much extra space to carry things. But like the bulky anorak man, the rucksack man quickly became tarred with society's misconceptions. Before long, he too became a figure of pity and morphed into sad fuck rucksack man. Sad fuck rucksack man always carried an absurdly coloured rucksack which never matched anything he wore. He usually carried too many things in his rucksack, and sometimes looked like he was transporting the chopped up body parts of a close family relative. Or latterly, the DIY online components for a latest terrorist outrage. When it rained and he was lugging his load down a main shopping thoroughfare, sad fuck rucksack man resembled a slightly demented, non-French speaking Quasimodo impressionist. Sad fuck rucksack man rarely looked like he was overburdened with a healthy bank balance. And, always seemed to have a lot of spare time on his hands. And this invariably led to 'rucksack skirmishes'.

In his day, Roddy was a constant victim of rucksack skirmishes. He'd enter Red Rock West. He would be flicking disinterestedly through the bargain CD section and he would try to turn when from behind, another sad fuck rucksack man – who looked like his rucksack was stuffed with two other rucksacks – would be trying to turn simultaneously and both rucksacks would become entangled. Both sad fuck rucksack men would delicately try to manoeuvre out of their trapped positions. This would take some time, amidst much intermittent low cursing and embarrassment.

Bookshop aisles were also a fraught area for potential rucksack collisions. Roddy had lost count of the amount of times he would be browsing in a bookshop and he would see another sad fuck rucksack man approaching. Suddenly, both would be intertwined together and a painstakingly delicate operation of gradual unlocking would commence and eventual freedom would ultimately be achieved. But only after half the books from the middle shelf of the Biography section had come tumbling to the ground. As Roddy would look down on the assembled titles, he'd wonder, when did bookshops begin putting the biographies of serious historical figures next to cheesy comfy risible TV figures? Marshall Tito next to Alan Titchmarsh? Truly the world is doomed.

Cafes were the worst. Roddy always seemed to bump into another sad fuck rucksack man entering a café, just as he was leaving. Rumour had it that the fire brigade once had to be called a few years back when two overweight sad fuck rucksack men got wedged in the doorway of a coffee shop on Prospect Hill.

With the money Agnes had given him for his recent forty-fourth birthday, Roddy decided to replace his rucksack with a brand new manbag. A beautiful dark brown leather number with the obligatory *has been lying in the scorching Mojave Desert for over five years* look. However, once he had bought the manbag, almost immediately he felt an acute sense of buyer's remorse. He kept putting off having to wear it into town. Or carry it into town. Roddy thought it was always a bad sign about an item if you were not sure which verb to use when describing what you actually do with it.

He felt deep down that maybe he wasn't really a manbag sort of person. Modest shoulder frame. Lacking in height. The best summation always has been short and squat. He'd always been suspicious of manbags. They are as much a uniform for slightly non-conformist creative people and other chancers as pin-striped suits are for bankers. But living in an era of self-image obsession Roddy reluctantly had to accept that the orange magenta rucksack had to go. And every time he visited Agnes recently, she would ask 'How's the manbag?' or she'd say 'Haven't seen you with that manbag, yet,' or somewhat poignantly, 'There's an old jacket of Ger's, the Lord have mercy on him, still lying around that would probably look great with that manbag!'

One afternoon, Roddy decided to finally bite the bullet and make a low-key dress rehearsal sortie into town with the manbag. He'd been walking for five minutes when a bird shat on his manbag. But that wasn't too bad, he figured, it just added to its authentic faded worn out appearance. After about an hour he felt a twinge in his left upper trapezius shoulder muscle. Which made no sense as he had very little in his manbag. His biro and small notebook, a bargain-priced *Being John Malkovich* DVD, two parsnips and his reading glasses (a recent development) and glasses case but he still felt like one of Santa's little helpers lugging around prospective Christmas presents. These manbags aren't great for transporting items. He needed a break.

As he stared down on his cup of coffee in one of those funky, recently opened establishments, where the position of the coffee cup is perilously close to the edge of the saucer, and surrounded by other manbag owners, impersonating Zen zombies as they gazed down benignly on their device of choice, he wondered was it possible to source another orange magenta rucksack on eBay? He realised that you can't stop being who you are, and that by middle-age you are stuck with you. He knew he'd always be a rucksack man. Even an anorak man. But, in a million years, never a manbag man.

WAITING FOR PJ

Another new coffee shop is about to close for the day. All they can offer Roddy Bodkin is a coffee-to-go. His need for a caffeine fix overpowers his loathing of the whole coffee-to-go culture and he reluctantly nods as he waits for his cardboard cup to be filled.

Two minutes later, he is standing on a street corner sipping his half-full cup of coffee-to-go, when a passerby, noticing him, takes out some coins and drops them into his cup. Roddy is gob-smacked. He calls after the passerby.

'Hey!'

The passerby turns.

'Yes?'

'Do I look like a vagrant to you?'

The passerby looks at Roddy and pauses.

'Kind of. Yeh.'

'You've just ruined my cup of coffee-to-go.'

The passerby shrugs his shoulders and walks on. Roddy begins to fish out the coins. Burns his fingers. Ow! Finally finds four euro. Not bad. In fact, very decent. Roddy regrets being so aggressive with the passerby.

This will cover the week's lotto ticket before going on to meet forthright farmer scribbler poet and drinking companion, Ambrose Hegarty, in PJ's. Tonight they are going to propose to PJ their Truly Awful Comedy Club idea.

Roddy enters the bar. Nods at Ambrose. Ambrose gripes.

'PJ's night off. Typical. Although, they say he might be in later.'

Roddy orders a pint and sits next to his buddy.

'Anything strange?'

'No. Stayed in last night. Watched part of an old Western on TG4.'

Roddy pays for his pint. Ambrose shakes his head.

'Never understood those Westerns. A cowboy is travelling for three days through the scorching Arizona desert. He eventually finds a small town, is parched with the thirst, positively parched, nearly falls off his horse and just about makes it into the saloon and goes up to the bar. And what does he order? A tiny shot of whiskey! That's what! A tiny shot of whiskey. Makes absolutely no sense.'

Ambrose takes a gulp from his foamy pint.

'Thankfully, I found a good documentary instead, on another channel, about the Nazis.'

Roddy wonders aloud. 'What would they make documentaries about if there'd never been Nazis?'

Ambrose doesn't hear him as he is all set to expatiate on one of his favourite topics.

'To be honest now though I wasn't crazy about the auld Krauts. I mean Hitler was a bit of a clown as far as I was concerned. And what I never understood was, I mean, he was always going on about this so-called Aryan purity, big blond blue-eyed fellas, but did he ever have a look at himself? A miserable straggly little fella with the silliest auld moustache. How far from the toned, muscular, fair, Teutonic warrior can you get?'

Ambrose Hegarty has made a valid point about Hitler. Trouble is Roddy has heard it many times before.

'I think Hitler was the Elvis of dictators. Stalin was the Jerry Lee Lewis of dictators. Franco? Now, I couldn't take him seriously. Not in the same league as the other two. The Shakin' Stevens of dictators.'

Roddy nods. He's heard that one, too. At least Ambrose hasn't started banging on about the Shining Path and the Tamil Tigers yet. But it's early in the evening!

See, that's what male friends do after many years. They meet up in pubs and have the same conversation. Many years ago, when the world of vinyl ruled, Roddy had come up with the theory that friends are like favourite record albums. And conversations with friends are like favourite album tracks. But eventually a person gets bored listening to those same album tracks. Marlon Brando was about to make an appearance.

'If Hitler was the Elvis of dictators then Marlon Brando was the Elvis of actors. First you had the great mould-breaking early period of the 1950s. Then the slide into mid-career mediocrity. Then his Elvis 1968 television comeback phase with *The Godfather* and *Last Tango in Paris* in the early 1970s leading finally to the couldn't-care-less fat slothfulness period ending in terminal decline and overdue demise.'

Roddy bows his head slightly. Partly in agreement. Partly in boredom. There is a pause in the conversation. Roddy stares at a woman, taut compact body, swarthy complexion, ordering a drink at the bar. Ambrose notices her too. He edges a little closer to Roddy, as if plotting a conspiracy.

'I was always a great man for that dark exotic look. Michael Caine's wife now, jays she is a fine thing. Or Maria Callas. That Greek look. Or the Spaniards. Penelope Cruz. Or the Italians. Sophia Loren. Jays, you can't go wrong with Sophia. That North African Mediterranean look, that's the one I always liked, like yer wan over there. Jays, when I first got the internet wasn't I surfing all those porn sites for about six months.'

Ambrose sighs. Then continues.

'Eventually it gets you down, though.'

Roddy nods. 'I know. The sordid exploitation of women. I think it has gone on for far too long. I feel things are changing though and the twenty-first century will be the century of the woman.'

'Arey, what are you on about? I'm not talking about that! Pornography makes you realize what a small willy you have. Jays, I couldn't walk down the street anymore knowing there are all those fellas out there in porn movies with gigantic cocks. I mean, Jesus Christ, it's inhumane to put the rest of us through that. Highly insensitive. It gives a fella an enormous inferiority complex. Why don't all those media commentators who are always writing about the emasculation of the man in early-twenty-first-century Ireland, why don't they write about porn-related Small Willy Syndrome and the fierce inferiority complex that comes from it.'

Suddenly, Roddy has a query.

'By the way, in your extensive research, have you ever come across a Dutch porn star called Ruud Bonk?'

'Ruud Bonk? No. Don't think so. Why?'

'Nothing.'

The swarthy compact woman collects her drink and joins her friends in another corner of the bar. Roddy takes an extra big gulp from his pint and looks away from forthright farmer scribbler poet Ambrose Hegarty. A man with a hairstyle best described as failed-mullet, who has never completely mastered the art of inserting a belt in the belt-loop of his trousers. Still, he is a good friend. A very good friend.

'Before I had the computer at home Roddy, I'd go to the internet cafe to surf the porn. But that was like the old days. I'd be surfing but I'd feel self-conscious like someone was looking over my shoulder, the same way you were in a shop having a peek at those porn magazines when you were young.'

Roddy momentarily perks up. 'What porn magazines? There were no porn magazines in Ireland in the 1980s!'

'There was too! One. *Executive*. They published

it for four weeks. It was like a porn magazine except the models kept most of their clothes on. In most porn magazines, first page she has her clothes on, third page she doesn't have her clothes on, but in this magazine first page she had her clothes on, third page she still had her clothes on. No wonder it failed miserably in the marketplace.'

Roddy sighs. And looks at his watch. Ambrose is particularly talkative tonight. Wish PJ would turn up.

'Of course before *Executive* you'd have a peek at the auld *National Geographic* magazines. Now and again. Just to see, like, you know. Those tribes, like, in Africa. The ones where wearing clothes isn't a priority. I was one of the few people who enjoyed going to the dentist when I was growing up because he'd always have a few *National Geographics* lying around. I'd pretend to have a toothache just to go there. See this tooth here?'

Roddy reluctantly peers into Ambrose's mouth.

'What tooth?'

'Exactly. Sometimes you have to suffer for your obsessions. Then there were those artsy coffee table books in O'Gorman's bookshop on Shop Street, with photographs of Parisian prostitutes, in fishnet tights, taken about 1907. I mean you'd see a fair bit of flesh like, you'd see it *all* like, but jays, there'd be something spooky about looking at naked people who are long dead, like you know, didn't enjoy that at all, but sure what could you do like, you were starved for a bit of stimulation, like you know. I mean there was nothing on the telly. Except when the continuity announcer would announce a film and sometimes warn that some viewers might find some scenes offensive. Jays, you'd pray for one of those announcements. And hope mammy and daddy weren't in the room. But then you'd sit through the movie for two hours and there'd be nothing in it. You might catch a glimpse of Brigitte Bardot's naked *back* if you were lucky!'

Ambrose looks sadly into his pint.

'Brigitte Bardot. Sylvia Kristel. Those Continentals, jaysus, they are so natural about their bodies. Walking around naked all the time... Not like we Irish, we're so self-conscious about our bodies... Well my generation anyways, not like the young ones today getting up to no good... I've got this theory about it. It's called my 'Reluctant Nakedness Theory'. We Irish got the worst of both worlds. Eight hundred years of the British telling us to have reserved stiff upper lips and not to show our emotion and hug people, and on top of that we had fifteen hundred years of the Catholic Church telling us not to touch our genitalia. (*They* were allowed to touch our genitalia mind you!) So we've had decrees from two different authority structures. The British people only had the one. But they were Protestants so it was OK for them to have sex, I suppose. And the Catholics down in Spain and Italy, sure jaysus it was so hot down there they had to disregard church teaching eventually and strip to the bone, but here we were stuck up in cold damp northern Europe, with a lethal combination of both traditions that have shaped us and ensured our bodies are touch-free zones. Maybe, that's all in the past, but of course, now we are too old to be having the fun. Dreadful days, Roddy. Dreadful. Still getting over them. If I read one more article about the age Irish people, nowadays, are having sex, and all the partners they have, I'll scream! We missed out on the good times, Roddy, we missed out on the good times.'

Roddy sighs in agreement. He then sees PJ waddle in. If PJ was in the mafia he'd be known as PJ Four Bellies.

'PJ's here.'

Ambrose stands up. Followed by Roddy.

'Howye, PJ, could we have a quick word with

you?'

PJ totters to an unoccupied side of the bar.

'Sure, lads, what is it?'

The pitch about the comedy club goes very well. They have the upstairs room and bar for the night of Wednesday, October 2nd – doors opening at 8.30. Roddy is a little disappointed it isn't the previous Wednesday, September 25th, because of his Comedy Covenant deadline of September 30th but he'll only miss it by two days. Two days! Not bad for a man not great with deadlines. Take a bow, Roddy Bodkin. His comedy career *will* finally be launched around the time of his self-imposed cut-off date. Seven weeks away. Lots of time for preparation. And getting those quarter-formed ideas into shape. PJ will keep the bar take. They won't charge in at the door but pass a bucket around at the end. And Roddy and Ambrose promise to handle all the publicity. After that, they'll see how it goes. PJ queries The Truly Awful Comedy Club as the name of the event but lets it pass. 'I suppose ye know what you're doing.' He also stipulates one more condition. His son Eoghan is in a ZZ Top tribute band called The Counterfeit ZZ Top. PJ wants them on the bill. So they can get a gig. Somewhere.

‘What are they like?’ Ambrose inquires.

‘Between meself and yourself. Brutal. But you’ll be doing me a favour.’

‘No problem PJ. We love brutal.’ Roddy replies. ‘In fact, I think The Counterfeit ZZ Top will fit right into The Truly Awful Comedy Club.’

THE BROTHER

Saturday morning. Roddy Bodkin's younger brother Ronan is in town having a coffee on Dominick Street. Reading the newspaper. Trying to enjoy his 'downtime'. Is downtime just an expression for your own free time, or your own free time while you are also feeling down? Because Ronan is feeling down and isn't enjoying his downtime. He keeps re-reading an article about another possible outbreak of the cryptosporidium parasite in Barna but cannot maintain his concentration.

He'll have to pick up Ciaran in a half hour from football practice. Go out to Kinvara. To see mother. So much for downtime. He can't relax. Feeling the pressure. Himself and Jenny never have time for each other anymore. He's busy with work. Natural wood flooring took quite a hit with the financial crash a few years ago and is still not back to pre-2008 figures. He can't switch off. He gets home. He's knackered. The kid is great, though. Nearly thirteen, now. Agnes loves the kid. And Ger did too. Dad loved that kid. So glad Dad lived long enough to see the kid. His only grandchild. At least the family name will live on. That's what Ger said to him six months before he died. The family name will live on. Thank God. Your older brother – well you can forget about that clown – but you, you have ensured that the family name will live on. A Bodkin with our genes, Ger said, raising his fist. We will live on. We won't die out.

When he gets out to Kinvara, mother will ask why not have another one?

Not just up to me, he'll reply. Agnes will continue, we couldn't have that many because of my complications in the endometrium but we wanted to, as your father, the Lord have mercy on him, told you many times, we wanted to badly, but you were a late child, very late, not an unwanted child, a blessing, God, no love and we were so proud of you too, at least we didn't get you in the wind, like that other fella, but it is one of my biggest regrets in life only having the two, but you and Jenny, both of you are still young, both hundred-percent healthy, not like me with that complication, and now all those other complications, why not have another one, one isn't normal, one is more normal than none, none is inexplicable, but that's your brother for you now, and he's set out his stall, but one isn't normal. Give Ciaran a little brother or sister. It's Jenny, isn't it? I don't want to do her down, but, God knows, she lacks the motherly thing sometimes. Busy with the bit of teaching and her own little ventures and that bit of baking she does on the side for that farmer's market or what have you. I don't want to be bad-mouthing her because she is your wife and my daughter-in-law and myself and your father, the Lord have mercy on him, always had a lot of time for her but she could easily have another child. The two of you, with your income and if there was ever a problem which there won't be, because if I know my younger son as well as I think I do, there would never be a problem, but if there was, on the off chance in the future, you would have nothing to worry about. Nothing at all. There is money put away for a rainy day. I'll say no more.

Ronan ruminates some more about his mother. She tends to go on. But they are so alike. Both worriers. And he has so many things to worry about. All the time. Laminate and parquet flooring is now popular with the consumer, and sisal carpeting is experiencing a major renaissance. He was gutted last week when it was announced sisal is on the rise, big time, competitively-priced and sturdy, and customers were still passing on natural wood flooring, although he did find some glimmer of hope in the fact that the S-tech insulation efficient Nordic Beech flooring option was proving remarkably resilient in the North Leinster region.

Then of course there is climate change to worry about. The ice-caps are melting. Rain forests are being felled. More extreme weather events occur, year in, year out. He's struck by the way that, on TV, heatwaves are still greeted by smiling newsreaders and cheery weather forecasters. Broadcasting companies haven't made the adjustment. To them, sunny weather still equals a 'good news' story. No, it isn't a 'good news' story. Not anymore. Not spookily hot record-breaking temperatures sunny weather. It's a sign of the inferno to come! Ronan worries about that. He's a worrier. A genetic hand-me-down from Agnes. Agnes was always worried about things when he was younger. The Cold War. The Russians and the Americans annihilating each other. Palpitations about Brezhnev. She never stopped going on about it. What sort of ruined hairless planet would he grow up in? A lot of angry unemployed barbers and hairdressers out there in the future. She advised her niece, Mildred, in 1985 to forget about hairdressing. No future in hair after the nuclear holocaust. And now Ronan wonders about the world Ciaran will have to survive in.

He remembers as a child when Ger and Agnes went on holidays and he, younger than Roddy, was sometimes packed off to stay with relatives in Longford. Did he ever worry that something might happen to his parents and they'd never come back?

No. He automatically presumed they'd return. He misses that feeling of automatically presuming. Getting older is losing that feeling forever and becoming aware of all the things that can go wrong.

And don't get him started on Islamic terrorism. OK, Galway is not the Tora Bora caves, but you never know. There's always that threat. He heard one of Roddy's friends talk about Al-Qaeda once. Ambrose, what's his name? Geraghty, was it? Ambrose was almost in awe of them. You have to hand it to Al-Qaeda, he said. They are the best. The brand leaders. If they put their mind to something, they carry it out. They take it to a new level. Head and shoulders above the rest, that's what Ambrose said. They ended up drinking together. One night in The King's Head. Without Roddy. He never stopped talking about Al-Qaeda. And then he was off on a rant about how Al-Qaeda put the IRA in the half penny place. Will you ever go and fuck off about the IRA, he said. Sure those fellas never did any suicide bombing. Sure, we all can plant a bomb and make a phone call and all that shite, but Al-Qaeda, now they're the fellas, strap it round your ribs and detonate it – there's no flies on them fellas! Then this guy Ambrose listed some other terrorist organisations. Shining Path? Stupid feckin' name, I mean, like, what are they fighting for... Clean pavements? Just confuses people. The Tamil Tigers aren't bad now, I'd have a soft spot for them, but as for those feckers in Spain, ETA, the Basques, can't take them seriously. Amateurs. Killing a policeman in an underground car park in some deserted resort at two-thirty in the morning. Not exactly a 'spectacular' is it? I mean if you are going to be killed in a random terrorist atrocity, you want to be killed by the best and in my book the best, by far, streets ahead of everyone else, are Al-Qaeda!

That Ambrose. What a head-the-ball! Ronan smirks slightly. He then sighs as his thoughts are clouded with worry again. What about the lone unhinged wacko with a grudge? There has never been a high school massacre in Ireland. But with the predominance of American culture it is bound to happen sometime. Of course it would be the school Ciaran goes to. But how can you protect the kid from all that possible danger? Keep him at home all the time? No wonder he, as a concerned father, is worried. His stand-by mode is one of gnawing dread. Quivering innards. What's wrong with him? He needs help. But he's not going to talk to some eejit psychiatrist sitting there nodding. But sometimes he does get into one of his 'moods'. Like the brother. Like the father. Fathers pass on eyebrows, which soccer team to support, and the 'moods'.

It's probably causing him that other problem. His maintaining issue. His sustaining issue. Fuck it, his erectile dysfunction issue. Jenny is very understanding about it. And according to all those websites it's a temporary condition. Yeh, but five months, three weeks, two days and ten hours is a long temporary.

It all started during their weekend away in Paris after Easter. Don't worry about it, Jenny said, it happens to most men. Wait a minute? How many men with erectile dysfunction has my wife attempted to have sex with? Stop it. She was just trying to be nice. But he did worry about it. Preyed on his mind. And that sense of assuredness went and before he knew it, when they got back to Galway, it happened again. Then it began happening regularly. Then it began happening all the time. Then he started putting off conjugal evenings. Drank too much. Developed headaches. Told Jenny he had an important meeting the following morning – which he did, Jesper and Henning, representatives from the head office of Nordberg Natural, were coming in from Denmark – but Christ he was a man, and a man should be available any time of the day or night for some rumpy-pumpy. He used to be such a walking, throbbing, loving machine. And now this? If only he could stop all this negative thinking! No wonder he never enjoys his downtime.

He looks at his smartphone.

Is it that time already? Better go pick up the kid.

THE BLISTERINGLY FUNNY SHIT-HOT COMEDY MATERIAL

Only a few weeks left until the Truly Awful Comedy Club gig. Roddy opens his small notebook. He reviews his complete output since his self-proclaimed Comedy Covenant the previous September. Ten jokes. Ten miserly jokes. In ten months! What a disgrace. Not good enough. Has to do better. Shocking. That's what it is. Absolutely shocking.

Why can't he write more stuff? He started too late, that's why. His brain hasn't been trained to 'write funny'. Also, he didn't have the proper comedic influences as a child. As an impressionable comedy-loving youngster in the Galway of the late 1970s and early 1980s, what influences were there?

Only RTE television.

No wonder he's fucked.

Roddy watched only one TV channel until he was nine years old. RTE One. And the main comedy that channel showed were movies with Eddie Cantor. Will Hay. The Marx Brothers. Danny Kaye. Harold Lloyd. Red Skelton. Laurel & Hardy. In other words – ancient stuff. Roddy Bodkin's formative comedy education and influences are seventy to eighty years out of date.

Being stuck in one-channel land stunted his growth and development as a comedy practitioner. And even when the second channel, RTE Two, appeared in November 1978, it showed more of the same. Charlie Chaplin. Bob Hope. Abbott & Costello. The Three Stooges. Norman Wisdom. Jerry Lewis.

In this litigious-friendly era he sometimes considers retrospectively suing RTE and the Irish State for denying him the right, as a then-impressionable comedy-obsessed youngster, to see more modern (for those days) comedy on television like Peter Cook and Dudley Moore. Monty Python. Chevy Chase. Rik Mayall. Richard Pryor. Rowan Atkinson.

The fact is, Roddy wasn't exposed to any up-to-date comedy influences. Not like today's kids. If they are interested in comedy or love a comedian, they can watch all his or her best stuff on YouTube. But back in those days? Very few contemporary comedians on Irish television. OK, there were a few 'home-grown' acts like Brendan Grace, Hal Roach and Noel V. Ginnity but Ger strictly forbade Roddy to watch them. 'I can't look at those fellas,' Ger would say, in a soft tone of voice that sounded like he'd just witnessed a gruesome car crash. 'I'm sorry, we have to turn off the television.'

So, it is not all his fault that his comedy output has been so derisory over the last ten months. He previews what he has come up with.

November 14th 2012: *When I was a child and did something bold, my mother used to hit me with a wooden spoon. I spent a lot of my childhood walking around with my trousers covered in flour, raisins, and almond paste.* Not bad, he thinks. Although, would today's audiences relate to the concept of the wooden spoon as an instrument of corporal punishment? Also, parents are no longer legally allowed to reprimand their children physically. And mothers? Do they cook that much for their children anymore? In this day and age, is it automatically right to assume that a mother should do the cooking for her child? What if she has a fulfilling career and is extremely busy? Why shouldn't father cook? Not sure if this joke will work.

December 21st 2012: *In the late 1980s, as a young fella, I was picked up in London on terrorism charges. Put in jail. I wrote to Margaret Thatcher to proclaim my innocence. I've got the letter right here. 'Dear Mrs.*

Thatcher, you know until the age of fourteen, I thought babies came out of belly-buttons. I mean, is that innocent or what?' That's funny. However, it is sort of related to things that happened a long time ago. Who of today's younger generation that go to comedy gigs, remember the Birmingham Six or The Guildford Four or Margaret Thatcher? Will have to look at that one again.

January 3rd 2013: *I don't like women who lead you on. Like last week I met this woman, and we were getting on well, you know, so she asked me my name and I told her. She wanted to know where I lived, so I told her. She wanted to know my phone number, I thought, OK, pushy, but I told her. Then she wanted to know if I was married or single, I thought, wait a minute, let's get to know each other first, go on a few dates like, anyway I eventually told her I was single. Then everything just petered out, and she told me to take a seat, the consultant would see me presently.* Hmmm. Male-female interaction is quite contentious nowadays. Women leading men on is debatable subject matter in this whole era of sexual assault and date rape and justifiable criticism of the ongoing patriarchal structures of society. I'll set that one aside for the time being.

February 18th 2013: *Years ago I was so depressed I tried to kill myself. I tied a rope to the lightbulb in my bed-*

room. Put the noose around my neck. Got on a chair and jumped off. Nothing happened though. The bedside lamp just fell off the bedside table. Making light of mental health issues? Not a good idea. Somebody in the audience might have been depressed or a family member may have committed suicide. You just don't know nowadays. Don't think I can try this one out.

March 23rd 2013: *I always wanted to be a jazz musician but the triangle isn't a jazz instrument.* That's quite funny. Although, are young modern metropolitan audience members tuned into jazz and authentic early-to-mid-twentieth-century Americana?

April 15th 2013: *If every cloud has a silver lining how come it never rains tin foil?* A bit surreal. Not bad. Could work.

June 5th 2013: *Originally, there were five Beatles. John, Paul, Sartre, George and Ringo.* Do audiences today know who Jean-Paul Sartre is? Do they know who the Beatles are? Note to myself. Need to start writing more up-to-date stuff. Will do some cursory online research on Beyoncé.

July 30th 2013: *Crime in multi-storey car parks. It's wrong on so many different levels.* Ha ha. Ha ha. Ha ha. Ha ha. Great joke. That'll work. Have them in stitches. How did I come up with that one? Wait a minute. I didn't come up with that one. That's someone else's joke. That's a Tim Vine joke. Heard him doing it on the TV a few years back. Fuck. And it was such a good one. Wait. Will people know? The audience wouldn't know. Maybe I could sneak in a stolen joke or two. Be a covers comedian, like Cormac Creedon was for a while. Just at the beginning. To get me started. No. No. Must have comedy integrity from the word go! Has to be deleted from the list.

August 5th 2013: *I hate it when you look up a builder's website and it says 'currently under construction'.* That's a good one. No problem with that one. That's sure-fire. Topical reference. Sort of. Websites under construction. They'll like that one. Will end with that one. Trouble is, what'll come before it? A joke about playing jazz on the triangle and a one-liner about tin foil?

Roddy realises he has only three jokes.

Wait a minute. He has an idea. Could be a great idea! He feels some blisteringly funny shit-hot comedy material coming on. Where's the biro? Can never find a biro when you need one. Found one. Have to write this down.

I think some words from the Irish language would sound great spoken by the Mafia during arguments. Im-

agine a scene from The Sopranos or a Martin Scorsese movie.

'Hey Vito? You know what you are?'

'What?'

'You're nuthin' but a Modh Coinníollach.'

'What the fuck are you calling me?'

'I'm calling you a Modh Coinníollach.'

'What the fuck is a Modh Coinníollach?'

'It's what you are. It's what your mother is. It's what your father is. It's what you're whole fuckin' family are! You're all nothing but a bunch of Modh Coinníollachs!'

'What did you say to me?'

'I said what I said. It is what it is. You're nothing but a bunch of mooks. You're nothing but a bunch of mommalukes. And you're nothing but a bunch of Modh Coinníollachs!'

Roddy sits back and basks in his brilliance. He feels this routine will be his passport to regular comedy employment. There's just one minor problem, though. He'll really need to start working on that attempt at a New York accent.

KISSING WITH CONFIDENCE

Every time Roddy hears the 1984 Will Powers song 'Kissing With Confidence' on some oldies radio station, he is reminded of the bad breath he experienced during his teenage years and he immediately begins to hiccup incessantly for two hours. The song evokes such horrendous memories that it triggers a complete collapse. A nightmarish aural subversion of Proust's madeleine cake. An unwanted revisit into the hellish universe that was awkward adolescence and teenage discos.

Noreen, an old acquaintance from his days at Fleming Travel, has always liked him and he has been told by a mutual friend that he should call her up. After the non-date with Fiona he's a little reluctant but he already knows Noreen has the 'hots' for him and to be honest he'd love a night (OK, maybe nine minutes) of unbridled (settle for bridled) passion. He hasn't had a sexual encounter since that ill-fated 'kitchen worktop position' fiasco with Lorraine. He kept explaining to Lorraine that he was never great with stretching and lifting and getting 'angles of entry point' correct. In fact, geometry was one of his worst subjects in secondary school. But Noreen is probably quite traditional. If memory serves him correct she is from Crossmolina in County Mayo. Nowhere more traditional than Mayo. Given the devout nature of the place, and the ongoing popularity of Mother Teresa up there, he is convinced Mayo people probably only ever practice the 'missionary' position. And that suits Roddy just fine. Could do with a bit of run-of-the-mill mating ritual predictability – especially after the near-crazy goings on with that Dutch couple! Yes. He will ring Noreen.

The phone call is made. The date is set up, enthusiastically and almost immediately, after some banter about mutual friends and the past. This must be how those big comedy stars feel, Roddy reflects. They already know that the person they call likes them before they ask them out. Kicking in an open door. If only life was always like this.

Firstly though, he'll have to go into town and do some shopping. He's picked a simple pasta recipe from a Jamie Oliver book Ronan gave him as a present in 2005.

A solitary tin whistler is busking as Roddy walks down Buttermilk Lane. Being a student of authentic early-to-mid-twentieth-century Americana Roddy knows that the great Indiana-born songwriter Hoagy Carmichael had sung 'Old Buttermilk Sky' and because of this he has always liked the place name Buttermilk Lane, a nondescript rundown old historical laneway between Shop Street and Middle Street. The tin whistler seems to lack gusto, as if searching for the next note to play, but Roddy is in a good mood this morning and puts a fifty-cent coin in the busker's upturned leather cowboy hat on the ground.

Lost in thought, he walks past the Augustinian Church and suddenly a concerned mother warns her small son, peddling his bicycle unevenly on the footpath, to 'mind the man'. Roddy wonders when did *that* start happening? When did *he* become 'the man' in 'mind the man'? Seems like only yesterday that Agnes was warning him not to be knocked over by towering strangers. Now he's become just a middle-aged walk-on in that kid's morning. He sighs and admonishes himself for having such a dispiriting thought, then mentally pivots in a positive manner, and looks forward again to Noreen and the evening of possible libidinous hijinks ahead.

Roddy likes the idea of a date coming to his flat. Gives him a reason to attempt to tidy it. For once. Although, once he's back in the flat, he finds operating the landlord's hoover challenging, unpredictable and slightly dangerous. Like wrestling a baby giraffe.

Noreen arrives at eight o'clock on the dot.

Roddy finds her somewhat intense. But a very fast mover. They have hardly finished their main course of Jamie's tuna and black olives, with fresh basil leaves, shredded garlic clove in an arrabiatta sauce, washed down by a richly textured and full-blooded Campo Viejo Rioja 2011 when Noreen slinks up to him at his corner of the table.

'Tell me something about yourself that I don't know. Do you have any fantasies? Sexual fantasies.'

Jesus. So much for being traditional from Crossmolina. No one has ever asked him that question on a first date. By the end of his time with Lorraine, he had become somewhat bored with the light blue ostrich feather on the perineum manoeuvre so maybe it was time to confess to another particular fetish.

He answers Noreen's question directly.

'Ehm. I would love to be spanked by a leek.'

This intrigues her.

'Just the one?'

'Maybe two. Depends on their size.'

'Organic or supermarket?'

'Organic. It would be a more authentic experience.'

'And probably healthier.'

'Yes.'

'And nutritional. We could put them in some soup afterwards.'

Intense, fast, and, dare I say, someone who would excel at household budgeting, Roddy muses.

She unbuttons her blouse and purrs.

'Do you have a pantry? And if so, do you have any leeks lying around?'

A pantry? In this dive? Or maybe her use of the word 'pantry' is part of the role play. Roddy admonishes himself. He hasn't bought leeks for ages.

'Sadly, no, but I have rhubarb. I bought one the Wednesday before last. Rhubarb is fine too. Being spanked by a rhubarb.'

She moves closer.

'Well, let's get to it.'

She runs her finger down Roddy's v-neck sweater. Roddy feels a smidgen of a reaction in his crotch.

'OK.' Roddy says as he gets up from his chair.

He frantically roots for the rhubarb in the west wing of his box-sized flat in Palmyra Avenue.

Where can it be? You can hardly swing a cat in this place, or even a kitten, yet I can't find that solitary rhubarb.

Where did that expression come from anyway? You can hardly swing a cat in this place. So if it is a spacious abode, do people happily spend their days actually swinging handfuls of felines? Just wondering.

'Be a minute, don't worry. Bound to turn up somewhere.'

Roddy finally finds the rhubarb. Has shrivelled somewhat. Past its peak. But still firm enough for some playful buttock slapping.

He re-enters the kitchen. Or actually, he just turns around. The flat *is* that small.

'Found it. Still in reasonably good nick.'

She smiles. A skittish temptress in mauve.

'Shall we retire to the greengrocer's pleasure-dome, my lord?'

'The what?'

'Your bedroom.'

'Oh. Yeh. The role playing thing again. Greengrocer. Fruit. Rhubarb. Get it.'

Suddenly, her phone rings. Roddy instantly recognises the melody. And freezes. What are the chances of a woman originally from Crossmolina,

County Mayo having Will Powers' 'Kissing With Confidence' as her ringtone?

Two hours later, Noreen is long gone and Roddy is still sitting on his chair and hiccupping loudly.

CONVERSATION WITH DAD

It is the 16th of September. Ger's anniversary. Roddy is in Rahoon Cemetery. He makes his way over to Ger's final resting place. Just down from some nuns. Near that giant pylon.

'Hi Dad. How are things?'

'You haven't been here for a while.'

'No. Sorry. Been a bit busy. How are you getting on?'

'Arey, not great. Gets a bit lonely up here. But, we are where we are and I am where I am. Sure, what can you do?'

'How are the neighbours?'

'Quiet most of the time, the nuns are grand like, no one visits them, but your one, to the left, next to me had an awful lot of visitors during the last while. Jesus, they never stopped coming up to see her. What's her name, again?'

'Uh. Let me see. Bridget Concannon, née Cleary. Wife. Mother. Grandmother. Aged seventy-one.'

'Cleary. I wonder, was she one of the Clearys from Athboy?'

'Ronan was saying he thinks somebody might be stealing some of those gravel stones on top of your grave. Wouldn't put it past some people in this day and age. Never underestimate the mendacity of humankind, as you used to say.'

'Did I say that?'

'Regularly. What do you think about the gravel stones? Ronan thinks it also might be birds swooping down. Dodgy theory as far as I'm concerned. I mean, the birds swoop down and steal these special gravel stones and what do the birds do with these stones? Build little driveways in their nests?'

'Maybe it's the wind. Was howling a gale up here last Thursday night.'

'Don't think so. I spotted some missing gravel stones the last time I was here, also. I don't know what it is. I'm baffled but the stones keep disappearing. It is looking depleted.'

'Hadn't noticed. But, listen here, those plants you and Ronan planted six months ago, don't think you've cut them back lately.'

'No sorry, they are a bit unkempt. We'll have to do that soon. Ronan said he might be up next week to see you.'

'How's your mother? She hasn't been up in a while.'

'No. And with winter coming in she probably won't be. Anyway, it's a bit of a trek from Kinvara. And she's getting a bit forgetful. She's even stopped playing bridge. I'm a little bit concerned.'

'Really. Always sharp as nails Agnes. Then again, eighty this year. Getting on. Probably not much time left. She'll be on top of me any day now. Look forward to that. Agnes on top. That was always a rarity.'

'Dad, did you just crack a risqué joke about yourself and mother?'

'Yeh, I can say anything I want now. Doesn't make a blind bit of difference. Although, to be honest, with some of her people from the long forgotten days up in Forthill Cemetery, she was always moaning about having to end up in Rahoon.'

'United won on Saturday.'

'Oh. Who were they playing?'

'Crystal Palace. 2-0.'

'Who scored?'

'Eh, you wouldn't know any of the players, Dad. Sure, you've been dead for twelve years. I followed it on my new smartphone. '

'What do you mean?'

'The match. All the latest updates on my phone. Even watched the goals afterwards.'

'On your phone? What are you on about?'

'Remember that thing the internet, I was telling you about a few years ago.'

'Was that the thing about bread and cult leaders?'

'What?'

'Something to do with toast.'

'No. That was Twitter. I think what I said was Twitter is when a person takes a photo of a toasted avocado sandwich and shares it with their followers.'

'Sounds like bread and cult leaders to me.'

'Anyway, the internet is something much bigger. You can watch things, read stuff, book flights and buy shoes. Do almost everything online now and on your phone. You can even watch a football match on your phone.'

'Watching football on your phone. Sure, Jesus tonight, you could hardly see it. What's the point?'

'It's called progress, Dad. Allegedly. And it's so easy to get the soccer results nowadays.'

'Yeh, it could take hours in the old days.'

'It certainly could. Do you remember Dad, when we tried to listen in to the results all those years ago, on BBC Radio Two? Five to ten at night, and the reception would be so bad, we'd have to strain to hear over the interference. No Aertel in those days. Or Ceefax. Or internet. We'd have to wait until five to ten. I could never concentrate on my homework, if there was a match on, wondering how United were getting on. You'd give out to me, but it was because of you I supported them. And the radio reception would be so poor we wouldn't be able to find out the result on BBC Radio Two so we'd have to wait until quarter past ten, and the sports bulletin on RTE Radio One, presented by Sean Óg Ó'Ceallachain.'

'Oh Jesus, I remember that fella with his unpronounceable name and his nasally voice.'

'Or sometimes it was that other guy, the other guy who you couldn't stand, Michael Ó'Muircheartaigh – still alive, it's younger he's getting – anyway, he would go through the results of every other sport before he got to, as he would call it, 'the cross-channel results'. Do you remember that Dad? It drove you nuts.'

'I do. Vividly. Athletics from Zagreb. Another glorious failure from another Irish athlete. An under-16's hurling match from Castlecomer. Abandoned. Show-jumping from Düsseldorf. Eddie Macken would fall off his horse.'

'We didn't give a damn about that stuff, did we,

Dad? We wanted to know how United got on. But they kept us waiting. A report on some camogie game from Macroom. News from the basketball five-a-side championship in Drogheda. School swimming championship from Carlow. Items on snooker, darts, rugby, sailing, horse racing. But we'd still have to wait for those 'cross-channel results'. Then he'd go to the League of Ireland results.'

'Don't get me started, son! Don't get me started! You're right. Finn Harps versus St. Patrick's Athletic. We couldn't give a fiddling fuck. We don't want to know about that fourth-rate league! And don't you dare, Sean Óg Ó Ceallachain, don't you dare go up North and tell us about Glentoran versus flippin' Cliftonville because we will completely lose the rag. Get to the English League results. I remember, son. We always had to wait until the very end of the bulletin.'

'The car radio was better, Dad. The reception on the car radio was always better. And most Saturday afternoons we'd sit in the car in the front of the house and listen to BBC Radio Two. Peter Jones and Bryon Butler. Remember those two, Dad? Snooty types. Foreign Office voices. But quality commentators. Do you remember the time we had to go down to the promenade in Salthill with the car? I think Dermot O'Toole came with us. United versus Liverpool. FA Cup semi-final replay. April 1979. For once, the reception was even poor in the car outside the house. We had to go and try to find a place where it was better. We ended up opposite the Western House on Salthill promenade. Jimmy Greenhoff scored the winner that night, Dad.'

'A journeyman. No Denis Law.'

'United got to the FA Cup final that year. But Arsenal beat them. We were so happy, Dad, that night opposite Western House. We jumped with joy when they beat Liverpool. I think we banged our heads against the car roof, from the inside. Do you remember that, Dad? Nice memories, Dad. Nice memories.'

'It's all we have, son, at the end of the day. The memories. Although beware of too much ruminating, all the same. It gets you bogged down in the end.'

'Good point. Listen Dad, eh, I'll be off now, meeting Ambrose, do you remember Ambrose? We're meeting about a comedy thing we're organising.'

'What comedy thing?'

'I'm finally doing a comedy gig next month. A

bit of stand-up comedy.'

'You're not still going on about that auld stand-up comedy, are you? Sure you were talking about doing that years ago.'

'I know I was, Dad. But it's now or never. I've just turned forty-four. Don't want any regrets. At least I can say, I tried it.'

'I suppose, I understand. Life is like a cup of coffee after a meal, son. One minute it's there in front of you. Next minute, it's gone. You're entering middle age, now. The road behind is greater than the road ahead. I tried taking up the piano again when I was that age. Do you remember that Casio keyboard I bought? I think I took it out of the box only once. Then, after a while, your mother stuffed it down the back of some cupboard.'

'She's still at that game.'

PUBLICITY STRATEGY

Roddy and Ambrose meet outside Dubray Books on Shop Street. They are planning to go and have a coffee to discuss the publicity strategy for The Truly Awful Comedy Club opening night. Two recent meetings had to be aborted, in two public houses, for a specific reason. An occurrence that happens regularly in Galway drinking establishments and that Roddy and Ambrose abhor. Something like this. You are with your drinking buddy. You have just started your third pint. You are 'settled in' for the night. Suddenly, an unannounced group of traditional Irish musicians magically appear in the corner of the pub and start to play an unwanted frenzied seisiún. The ear-shattering intrusive cacophony of the tin whistle, bodrán, fiddle and button accordion renders all conversation pointless. Pints must be finished swiftly and a quick exit engineered.

Roddy looks at Ambrose.

'Which coffee shop will we go to?'

'I have to go into the bookshop first.'

Ambrose walks into Dubray's and strides over

to the counter. He addresses the young man behind the till.

'Howye, listen eh, I'm Bosco Reddin, the poet, I'm here for a day or two. Do you want me to sign some of my books?'

'Sure. Your new one *From Holy Water to Tipperary Water – Poetic Reflections on a Changing Ireland*, is doing quite well.'

He pauses.

'For a book of poetry.'

Then smiles.

'I'll go to the shelf and bring you over a few. Customers love signed copies.'

The young man leaves the counter unattended as he goes to find a few Bosco Reddin poetry collections.

Roddy looks at Ambrose.

'Do you do this often?'

'Well, you know I haven't finished a poem since 1998. So, sometimes, just you know, to see what it's like to be a published poet, I pretend, like. It's not hurting anyone.'

'Aren't you worried they'll know you're not Bosco Reddin?'

'Do *you* know what Bosco Reddin looks like? Look, apart from the late lamented Seamus

Heaney, does anybody in this country know what any other feckin' poet looks like?'

The young man returns with some slim volumes.

'Here you are, Bosco.'

Ambrose grins.

'I brought my own pen.'

It is later.

They are in Curious Coffee, *another* new coffee shop, this time on Abbeygate Street. Servers? Young. Ambience? Loud. Coffee? Curious.

'I miss the Italian style coffee. It's all the auld Ethiopian shite at this stage.'

'You can't really say that nowadays, Ambrose. People might think you're racist.'

'Will you ever go and feck off. I just don't like it. That North African coffee is fierce bitter!'

Roddy removes his glasses case and the small notebook from his newly acquired purple Kipling rucksack. Oxfam were very happy with that recently discarded manbag. He takes out his reading glasses and puts them on.

'Jesus, where'd you get those? You look like that painter fella, Hockney.'

'Yeh. I'm not crazy about them. Anyway, let's go through the checklist. Uhm, the cameraman for the YouTube promotional video?'

'Yeh, well I finally talked to Emer and she said Aonghus is off working in Canada at the moment, so eh...'

'Oh. OK. No Aonghus. Cameraman still needed. Unless I do something on the smartphone. I emailed Galway Bay FM a few times, trying to get an interview about the gig but they haven't got back to me.'

'I know a researcher there, but I don't think she likes me particularly.'

'OK, so still no progress on the YouTube video or radio coverage. OK, print media. I tried emailing *The Galway Advertiser* and *The City Tribune*, but again no one has got back to me.'

'Jesus Roddy, when *The Galway Advertiser* doesn't feel inclined to mention a gig of yours, you know you're a complete feckin' nobody.'

'Let's not lose heart. I'll try again.'

'Whatcha say? Jesus, it's mad loud in here.'

'I said we mustn't lose heart, Ambrose. I'll try again. Did you set up that Twitter account The Truly Awful Comedy Club@AwfulComedyClub ?'

'I swear. I spent five hours online last Tuesday morning trying to set it up. But I don't know what the fuck happened.'

'You mean nothing happened.'

'Yeh. I guess that's another one for the Things Still To Do list.'

Roddy pauses. Hip-hop music is blaring in the background.

'Now, I hope you concur but I've gone off Facebook.'

'Me too. I think they're dodgy. Totally dodgy.'

'OK, that's one thing we can take off the list. No Facebook.'

Ambrose scowls as he takes a slug of coffee. Roddy looks at him. He has an idea.

'What about good old fashioned posters and flyers?'

'What about good old fashioned money? That costs. Do we have a production budget?'

'Not on my salary from the museum.'

'Don't look at me. I'm a part-time farmer, former poet.'

'OK. Let's leave the promotion side for a while. What about the actual gig, Ambrose? You told me several times that you'd contact Cormac Creedon, or look out for him in McSwiggan's so you could get phone numbers for Eugene Thornton.'

Ambrose pours another sugar into his coffee. Roddy continues.

'Jeez, the more I think about it, maybe we'll give Eugene a miss. In this day and age. He probably doesn't want to resurrect Mustafa Drink anyways. What about the others though? Dinny Bruce, Presto Mulligan and Billy O'Brien. Any movement on that?'

'I'm still working on it.'

'OK, now I want to remain calm but they need to be firmed up a... s... a... p, or The Truly Awful Comedy Club will be an evening of me introducing and re-introducing The Counterfeit ZZ Top.'

'Leave it with me, Roddy. Don't worry. How's the new material coming along by the way? Have you written any funny links and stuff?'

'The material is coming slowly. But I've got some good stuff on builders, jazz instruments, tin foil and uh... the Modh Coinníollach'

'The Modh Coinníolach?!'

Suddenly Roddy is deflated. He shakes his head.

'Maybe we should forget the whole thing. Are we nuts? The whole idea was ill-conceived. Look at me. A deadbeat Galwegian forty-something. Pursuing an impossible dream. It's all hopeless. This gig has 'unmitigated disaster' written all over it. If we ever do get those posters and flyers done up, that's all we need to print on them. Come see an 'Unmitigated Disaster' at PJ's Bar, Lower Salthill, on Wednesday October 2nd at 8.30.'

Ambrose pauses. Shakes his head. Tries the motivational route. A familiar motivational route.

'Did you ever hear of Gaudi?'

Roddy is exasperated.

'Yes! You told me about him months ago. He tried building a church in Barcelona. Never finished it. Walked out in front of a tram.'

'Yeh. But he never gave up, did he? He kept going. He kept doing it to the end. This is no time to throw in the towel. The venue is booked and the show must go on! Anyway, everyone has to start out somewhere! Even here in Galway. Sure Druid Theatre Company were playing to minus ten people in Chapel Lane for the first few years! And now look at them! A world-beating cultural export.'

There is another pause. Roddy sighs.

'I've fuck all material.'

'Don't worry. You still have just over two weeks. Anyways, listen, I've got some new stuff, if you're stuck. If you want to have a look at it. Just offering. '

'Thanks for the offer, Ambrose. Maybe I will. It's not more 'fierce conundrum' stuff is it?'

'No. Something completely different.'

They finish their coffees. They both root for coins.

Roddy finally mumbles, 'Will we go halves?'

WELCOME TO MIDDLE AGE

Roddy's job at the Fisherman's Museum is no more. The museum had to close after an investigation into the misappropriation of Údarás Na Gaeltachta funding. It was uncovered that Tessie was one of the main beneficiaries of illicit grants due to an intimate relationship with board member Maolsheachlann Ó'Súilleabháin. Over the previous few weeks, Roddy had noticed a large amount of money lying around and for a split second one afternoon when he was alone in the museum – another successful day repelling tourists – he was tempted. But then he started to think. He could never commit a crime in Ireland. Because if he was found guilty and his solicitor attempted to build up his character references for the judge, the solicitor would not be able to employ the usual examples, 'He is an integral part of his local GAA club.' Eh, no. Not a GAA member. 'He's a good family man.' No. No wife. No children. 'He partakes in much voluntary work in the community.' No, he keeps away from all that 'picking up discarded empty crisps packets along the canal' routine. So whatever temptation he had for stealing a few bank notes quickly passed when he realised the judge would not just throw the book at him but a whole library.

There is much 'lying in bed' in his drab accommodation in Palmyra Avenue. Early to bed, late to rise has become Roddy's new motto. Some nights he stays up and watches Sky News. One thing that astounds him, of late, is what he calls 'The Pouting Selfie Death Shot'. Over the last few years when a young woman dies tragically, in a car crash or terrorist attack or a murder, and it makes the TV news, the photo her family release to the media is always one where this unfortunate and unlucky individual is pouting playfully. He feels there is a definite disconnect between the tragic circumstances of the young woman's demise and 'The Pouting Selfie Death Shot' released by the family, especially if there is a sex crime dimension to the murder.

Roddy also watches lots of movies. One night recently, he watched a movie he had seen fifteen years previously. Paul Giametti had a small part. But when he saw the movie fifteen years ago he didn't know who Paul Giametti was. But now he does. 'Paul Giametti was in that movie before I knew who Paul Giametti was.' Roddy has invented a term for this occurrence. Actors who subsequently have become famous between the first time and the second time you have seen a movie. Retrospective Recognition. That sounds good. Yes. From now on he will refer to this phenomenon as Retrospective Recognition.

He is starting to talk to himself. A lot. Even on the street. One day, he bought a pair of mini earphones, just plugged them into his new smartphone and started engaging in a loud conversation with himself as he walked through Eyre Square. The indifferent Galway public were none the wiser. He shared the idea with Ambrose who thought it was inspired and immediately inquired about the cheapest mini earphones available. In fact, apart from Ambrose, Roddy's social life is very limited. The only texts he receives are from his new best friend, Vodafone, about deals – *Unlimited Vodafone to Vodafone calls and texts! 500 MB of data! Plus 100 international minutes!* – he isn't interested in, or reminders from physiotherapists or medical practitioners or hospital departments about appointments he has no intention of keeping.

This morning Roddy looked at himself in the mirror. Again. After completing his once-a-month-flossing-of-teeth. Or yoga for gums. As, yes you guessed it, Ambrose likes to call it.

The reflection still suggested Nick Nolte. But not in good nick... Nolte. In his face he could see an embryonic elderly gentleman staring back at him. This elderly gentleman had certain physical similarities to Ger. Hovering like a visual harbinger. A dark shadow. A ghost. Ready to make an appearance. Sometime. Soon.

Earlier in the morning Roddy had been shocked at the pool of drool on his pillow when he removed his pillowcase. He reflected momentarily on his drooling career. As a young baby, obviously, he drooled in abundance. But then he went through a disciplined minimal drooling period of about thirty years. A near drool-free existence. The halcyon days. Then one morning when he was about thirty-seven, he looked down on his pillowcase and noticed a map of the world dribbled there. Held up to the morning light, and from a different angle, it looked more like his very own Shroud of Turin fashioned by saliva.

There were other bed-and-decay related issues to fret over. The shedding of dead skin. All those rogue escapee hairs. The continued and alarming absence of a morning erection.

And the fatigue. With middle age, Roddy has

realised, a person becomes tinned fruit just out of a can. Completely drained.

To take his mind off matters he turns on the television. Some annoying chap with an annoying name, wearing a cravat is appearing on BBC Two, contemplating life.

'The older you get the more of your generation die. It's like those old American civil war movies or Napoleonic war movies. You and your generation are like a regiment. One of those regiments with thousands of soldiers who are ordered to walk towards the enemy. At first, the further back you are, only a random few die. But as you move closer to the frontline, more of you die, some in close proximity. But you keep progressing forward. You have no choice. And the shots keep ringing out. And more die. And soon there are not that many left standing in your regiment. But there is no escape. That enemy rifleman's bullet will get you sometime. That's the way I see it.'

The annoying chap with the annoying name – Sir Lionel Trevelyan-Totterdell? – guffaws despairingly in that hooray-harry over-the-top way repressed, Oxford-educated, upper-middle-class Englishmen do. Roddy turns off the television.

He decides to walk into town. A bright cold

crisp early autumn day. The sun is playing peek-a-boo with the lunchtime crowds and some hardy souls, imagining it is Naples in July, sit scrunched up on benches along the Corrib river walkway eating their takeaway lunch fare.

Roddy wanders. He walks past the main Galway hospital on Newcastle Road.

Maybe Roddy should go for that long-deferred check-up. But he never gets round to making the appointment. Or he continues making the appointment, hence all those texts, but never keeps it. On the plus side, he has recently ended his short-lived infatuation with cigarettes.

He is much more dutiful when it comes to dental appointments. Which of course makes perfect sense. The worst a dentist can tell you is that 'all your teeth will have to be removed but we have a lovely selection of silicone dentures for you to choose from'. But the worst a doctor can tell you...

Ger died of colorectal cancer in mid-September 2001. Roddy remembers the day Ger was diagnosed the previous January. All the family were around Ger's hospital bed. The consultant had just spoken. There was silence and shock. Ger had just been issued a death sentence. And all Roddy could think of was, *is colorectal cancer hereditary*? What are the percentages? He wanted to ask the consultant immediately, right there and then – remembering how difficult it is to get hold of a consultant once he leaves to go somewhere else in the middle of his rounds – but he figured it would be considered bad timing and he could justifiably be accused of complete self-absorption, so he didn't actually ask the question.

About eight years after Ger passed away, once he'd turned forty, it was suggested Roddy go for a colonoscopy. Roddy was not enthused by the idea. At all. At all. But reluctantly acquiesced after some worrying online statistical research on the hereditary nature of colorectal cancer. The last thing a hypochondriac needs. Twenty-four-hour broadband. Daily bulletins on all the things he could die from. And some other things, he'd never heard of, that he could die from. An appointment was made. An advisory letter was sent out. No food after lunchtime the day before. Or better still as little food as possible for the few days beforehand to reduce the eventual deluge caused by the mandatory intake of Klean-Prep.

Roddy entered the pharmacy and furtively handed the young woman the Klean-Prep prescription. After five excruciating minutes, waiting, she informed him 'We're all out of it'. On to the next pharmacy. Same outcome. More delay. And acute embarrassment. And the next. We'll have it in the morning, another young female assistant said. Everyone seems to be having colonoscopies this weather, she added, smiling sweetly.

I can't face going into another pharmacy and they are all out of Klean-Prep, Roddy thought. I'll give it a miss. That's what I'll do.

That was four years ago and he's never actually had a colonoscopy in the interim. Or a check-up. But each time, after visiting Ger in the cemetery, he thinks about it again. And then puts it out of his mind and just fritters away another day.

After passing Galway hospital he keeps walking, takes a right and finds himself in Shantalla. In the distance, he hears the otherworldly siren of an ice cream van. Broadcasting an ancient tune. A slightly spooky soundtrack of childhood summer mornings and just-back-at-school early autumn afternoons. You'd think after all this time ice cream vans would update their playlist. But then he realises none of the kids nowadays are familiar with Popeye The Sailor Man, so they would have no idea how antiquated the melody is in the first place.

Roddy re-directs himself, crosses the traffic lights at Cooke's Corner and strolls down Henry Street, heading back into town.

Finally, he decides to go into Charlie Byrne's bookshop.

After dawdling for a few minutes next to the Film & Music section, Roddy is forced to move elsewhere. He has noticed that most times he browses in a book shop, invariably an employee of the establishment will pick that particular time to crouch in front of him and either empty a shelf or re-stock a shelf. In the 1990s this was always a tiresome occurrence but what has made it truly unendurable over the last ten years is the unfortunate arrival of the loose fitting trouser and the subsequent resultant epidemic of exposed bottom cleavage. Roddy has lost count of how many tops of bottoms he has seen since the turn of the millennium. And frankly he is sick of it. He does not want his unsuspecting eye to accidentally catch a glimpse of what these posterior posers have to offer especially when he has noticed that one never sees an *attractive* person's bottom cleavage. Always, it is the plain person's bottom cleavage. And that goes for both sexes. In a way it makes perfect sense. After all, attractive people don't need to expose the top of their bottoms to get noticed.

The sun has come out. He journeys out to Salthill and goes for a walk on Salthill promenade. Nothing sums up the comical imperfection of life like a walk on Salthill promenade on a fine day. The feel-good azure sky. The caressing aural balm of the waves. And that decades old nasal-clearing pong of Galwegian effluent.

He has built up a thirst. A foamy pint of Guinness, not too cold, is called for. Wanting to steer clear of PJ's, as PJ would inquire how the publicity was going for the upcoming Truly Awful Comedy Club evening, he ends up in Killoran's. A mid-afternoon crowd of world-weary drinkers. All solitary unhappy middle-aged men having Mexican stand-offs with their past as the intense orange sun shines in one window. An Edward Hopper painting. With pints. Roddy catches his reflection in the mirror. Once more. That faint facsimile of Ger is still there, staring back at him. He looks like a ghost in a jumper. Drained of youth and hope. The puppy fat contentment has long gone and his features have hardened. As he clings to his pint he has the troubled look of man who kills pet budgies for kicks. He looks into space. For an instant. For an eternity.

THE REMOVALS MAN

Roddy Bodkin walks into Red Rock West. He always likes to spend time – in a fit of buyer's masochism – going into the music shop to see if the CDs and DVDs he has bought over the previous six months have been subsequently reduced in price. On this occasion he has found seven items that have been reduced. Total money lost, twenty-two euro. He curses under his breath. Then his smartphone rings. It is Agnes. More cursing under his breath. She usually rings the landline. But his smartphone? Must be family-related news. Family-related *bad* news.

'Roddy, your Uncle Tony died this morning.'

'Oh.'

'Ronan is up to his ears as usual. Running the company booth at a trade fair in Munich this week.'

Roddy sighs.

'And my rheumatism is playing up.'

'It's OK, it's OK, where's the removal?'

'Well, they don't know yet. He's just died. It'll be in Sligo. That's all I know. I'm just off the phone with Phyllis. It was quite...'

Roddy interrupts.

'Sudden in the end?'

'Yes. Suddenly. I'll ring you later when I have more details. Goodbye, love.'

Poor Uncle Tony. They are all finally dying out. In the last three years, seven of his uncles have passed away. Uncle Joe (suddenly), Uncle Frank (peacefully), Uncle Tony (suddenly), Uncle Roger (after a long illness bravely borne), Uncle Pascal (peacefully), Uncle Father Frank – long story, Roddy had two Uncle Franks, but Ger's older brother was also a priest, so to differentiate the two Agnes' brother was referred to as Uncle Frank and Ger's brother was Uncle Father Frank – (suddenly) and Uncle Charlie from Dublin (after a long illness bravely borne). Now, Uncle Paddy in London is the only one left. Ditto with the aunts. Two years ago there were six aunties still alive but in the meantime the grim reaper has visited Auntie Dolores (after a long illness bravely borne), Auntie Collette (suddenly), Auntie Kit (peacefully), Auntie Nuala (suddenly), Auntie Assumpta (after a long illness bravely borne) and of course Auntie Eileen (peacefully). Now, Auntie Phyllis in Sligo is the only one living.

Soon, like cinema ushers, his uncles and aunts will all be extinct. These shadowy austere figures in old black and white photographs. Those visitors to his house as a child. Those people who vaguely resembled his parents. They are all shuffling off. Exiting stage death. He has to ponder this. No more reluctantly showing up at family funerals. Or trying to *avoid* family funerals. He is part of this clan. These *are* his people. His tribe. And he must pay due respect. With age he has learned to be solemn. To behave correctly. No more displays of facetiousness. No more drinking too much whiskey and silent derision. He will go to Sligo, and attend both removal and funeral.

If only though...

If only though, he hadn't *seen* Uncle Tony, during his summer holidays of 1983, on that small farm, near Tubbercurry. In the corner of that barn. With that sheep. Wouldn't mind but Uncle Tony was already married to Auntie Phyllis for a year. Still, Auntie Phyllis had just given birth to first cousin Una. In some parts of the country, couples, even as late as the mid-1980s, had sex for the first time on a wedding night. Then, rather than perfecting their lovemaking and taking time to enjoy each other, sensually, over a prolonged period of time, their immediate aim was to produce a child. So things went from no sex, to very quick insecure sex, to no sex. Poor Uncle Tony and Auntie Phyllis. Obviously things weren't working out in the bedroom. But from what Roddy could ascertain on that bright sunny morning, things were progressing rather nicely in the corner of that barn. Don't think Uncle Tony was expecting Roddy to walk in. He turned around. Hirsute buttocks exposed. Caught *in flagrante* with one of the flock from that blackface mountain breed. Presumably female. Could have been male. Roddy didn't feel it was the correct time to garner such details. Uncle Tony quickly straightened himself and tightened his trousers. Roddy looked confused and embarrassed. The sheep of indeterminate gender remained inscrutable.

Some incidents are never referred to again. A person is caught doing something. Another person sees them. But both people act as if it never happened. It is easier that way. And so it was with Roddy and Uncle Tony. Although Ger and Agnes were quite surprised the following Christmas when a more-than-generous cheque fell out of a Christmas card addressed to Roddy and Ronan from Tony, Phyllis and Una.

It is late afternoon. Agnes again.

'The removal is Wednesday at five o'clock, in Coen's funeral directors of Tubbercurry and the funeral is the following morning in the church at ten o'clock. I'd go myself but I'd be afraid.'

'You'd pick something up on the way.'

'Especially this time of year.'

'Don't worry. I'll make sure I'll be there.'

'Thanks. You'll be representing the family.'

'I know.'

Early Wednesday morning. Roddy has stayed overnight in the house in Kinvara and is trying on his funeral suit. Agnes insists on a suit. In earlier times, Roddy preferred more casual wear for funerals. Under a big coat. Jumper. Zip-up top. Slacks. Who'd notice? Everyone will, Agnes would say. It has to be a suit, she'd insist. And a shirt. Not *that* shirt! And tie.

Tie? Ridiculous. He hasn't worn a tie for ages but with all these recent funerals and his persistent mother he has become quite competent with the knot again. Then there are the shoes. Must be real shoes, she says. *Real* shoes. Not those flippin' loafers! You mean the ones you wear once a year that give you a blister on your heel? And you bleed from the inside into those special thin socks you have to wear that go with the shoes? Who notices what shoes you wear at a funeral? Roddy asks. You'd be surprised, she replies. People are always noticing things. Now like a good fella put on those black shoes, and don't forget to polish them!

Historical military campaigns in Russia seem shorter than the crawling eighty-mile bus journey northward to Sligo. Roddy starts thinking about the afterlife and, if there is such a thing, will you be reunited with loved ones? What happens if there are certain loved ones you don't want to be reunited with? It would be nice to see them again, once in a while, but stuck with them for eternity? Cooped up with them for three days over Christmas drives you nuts! But this would be for eternity. Eternity is a very *very* long time. And *how* precisely does eternity work? Where are you staying? A house? Can you get out of the house a bit, go for a walk? Or is it some compound structure? Like an upmarket, celestial, manacle-free Guantanamo. And if you do get out of the house, or the compound, what happens if you bump into other people you don't want to bump into. Like old neighbours. Wanting to know your business. It's not fair. You die, thinking you've left all this stuff behind, and they're right there. All the old neighbours. Like Josie Foley. Snoopy Josie. From number thirty-eight. Always wanting to know your business. Would she be there? One more thing. What age are you in the afterlife? Are you the same age you were when you died? That's OK for Bix Beiderbecke, Jean Harlow, James Dean, or John Belushi but what about old people? Who wants to die at the ripe old age of eighty-five and then be eighty-five for eternity? That wouldn't be much fun! Would put you off dying.

Roddy arrives at the funeral home just before five o'clock. He is quite exhausted and his legs are stiff. The bus driver was a devoted Chris Rea fan. Roddy can take the thinking woman's bit-of-Geordie-rough for one or two songs, but not for three hours.

He goes up to Auntie Phyllis.

'Sorry for your loss, Auntie Phyllis.'

He delivers the line with a mature earnest sincerity. They hug briefly.

'Agnes sends her best. She'd be here but for a touch of the rheumatism.'

'I understand. Thanks for coming,' Auntie Phyllis says.

Roddy approaches Una.

'Sorry for your trouble, Una.'

Una nods sadly.

'Sure, what can you do?'

Roddy shrugs in empathy. Walks towards the open coffin. He looks at Uncle Tony for a moment. A yellow man in a blue suit in a brown box. Roddy look again. He thinks he notices something else. Is that an *erection*? Suddenly cousin Jimmy approaches. He nods at Jimmy. Jimmy looks at Uncle Tony in the open coffin.

'Jeez, he's looking well.'

Roddy stares at cousin Jimmy. The family member that sense forgot.

Jimmy continues. 'They've done a great job.'

Roddy sighs. Not with that noticeable protuberance.

Jimmy whispers to Roddy. 'He's gone to a better place.'

Where Jimmy? The Polynesian Islands? He's going nowhere. He's dead. Or maybe he *is* in an upmarket, celestial, manacle-free Guantanamo with Snoopy Josie Foley from number thirty-eight.

Jimmy pauses. Then comes the slight wet in his eyes, his subsequent discomfort in trying to suppress the getaway tears and the manic quivering of the lower chin. Jimmy is about to deliver his removals party piece. Roddy braces himself.

'The poor...'

Roddy stares at the floor.

'The poor...'

Roddy exhales tensely.

Jimmy continues.

'The poor... *kray-thur.*' He quickly wipes his eyes and then clears his throat, once again, with a contrived cough.

Two hours later. Back on the farm. An irate cockerel had chased Roddy in the farmyard when he was seven. And he had run for his life, begging his parents to come to his assistance. The indignity of childhood.

Ham sandwiches, coleslaw, currant buns and tea are served. Relatives mingle, tea is refilled, sandwiches are half-finished and memories and old yarns about Uncle Tony are unearthed. The time he cycled from Ballinasloe to Croke Park for the All-Ireland Football Final of 1956, only for his bike to be stolen during the match. Took him four days to get back to Galway. The time himself, Phyllis and Una won that family holiday to Butlin's in Mosney, but it rained every day. A self-professed expert on current affairs, the time he appeared on the television show *Quicksilver* with Bunny Carr in 1978 only to refer to the famous German terrorist group of the 1970s as The Bladder-Meinhof Gang.

Roddy has heard all these stories before. But this is new Roddy. Family-orientated Roddy. He smiles and is the model of decorum as he nestles his fifth cup of tea. Then Una offers him a glass of whiskey.

The rest of the evening is blurred. Talk, laughter, more memories, a trip to the bathroom, more talk, a dropped sandwich, more laughter, a spilled drink, even more talk and then suddenly, a moment of extreme clarity as a question is hurled from across the room.

'Roddy, you spent some time here on holidays in the early 1980s, have you any special memory of Tony?' cousin Jimmy inquires.

Four words lodge in Roddy's brain. Gift. Horse. Mouth. Sheep.

Here is the moment. This is an opportunity too good to pass. He knows there will be repercussions. But Agnes should stop sending him to these family funerals! But then he wonders, what family funerals? There are very few left. There won't be any more after Paddy and Phyllis. Soon Agnes will be gone, too. No longer telling him what funerals to attend. Maybe, there'll come a time when he'll miss all this.

'You must have one or two stories about Tony. Come on, Roddy.'

There is a long pause. Then he finally speaks.

'None I can recall.' Roddy replies. 'Although he did send me a very generous present just before Christmas in 1983.'

THE TRULY AWFUL COMEDY CLUB

A man walks on a small stage in a black dinner jacket, frilly white shirt and dark trousers. He clears his throat. He attempts to sing some opera. He is out of range and out of tune. He apologizes. He then announces he is going to take a pill. He removes a large white pill from the inside pocket of his jacket. He holds it up. And slowly, teasingly, puts it in his mouth. He picks up a glass of water from the stage floor, takes a gulp from the glass and swallows the pill. He then places the half-full glass of water back down on the stage floor. He pauses. Inhales and takes a moment. Suddenly, a woman in a crimson fleece nods sides-stage and some opera music starts playing from her laptop. The man suddenly begins to mouth perfectly to a Tosca aria and then mimes the intense vein-bursting emoting that is an essential part of any opera performance.

Roddy turns to Ambrose in the small bar area at the back of that upstairs room in PJs.

'What do you think of Placebo Domingo?'

'He'll do. I still wish you had allowed me to

contact Eugene Thornton though.'

Roddy and Ambrose have arrived early to make sure everything is in order for the big night. Two hours until the doors open at eight-thirty. Show to commence at nine. A hassled Presto Mulligan approaches them.

'You haven't seen a rabbit, have you?'

'No, sorry Presto.'

'We didn't think you did real tricks.'

'I always do real tricks. I'll have you know I won the Portlaoise Prestidigitator Of The Year Award in both 1989 and 1992.'

He scurries off shouting 'Rufus? Rufus, why do you always do this? We have to go prep that new trick. Rufus?'

There is some commotion on the stairwell. Items being transported. Male voices chatting, commenting and laughing, sounding closer as they ascend the steps. Finally, three bewhiskered guys in black cowboy hats enter. Roddy shakes his head in amazement.

'They really do look like ZZ Top.'

It is an hour later. Much pre-show nerves are in evidence and the tension is building.

Desperately aware he needs some extra material Roddy is trying to decipher some of that new stuff Ambrose has written. 'You know when you see a fella who always used to be thin and now he's fatter you think to yourself, oh, he's put on a bit of weight but if you see a fella who always used to be fat and now he's looking thin you think jeez, he's not looking too well, he might have cancer or something. Explain that fierce flummoxing quandary.'

Roddy mutters inaudibly to himself.

A quick tempo electric guitar suddenly growls in the background. Accompanied by a swift surging bass line and an eccentric drumbeat.

The intro takes its time, before some attempted harmonised vocals are heard.

'She's got legs, she knows how to use them.

She never begs, she knows how to choose them.'

The woman in the crimson fleece, still seated with a laptop, turns to Roddy and whispers.

'They may look like ZZ Top. But they certainly don't sound like ZZ Top.'

'Yeh,' Roddy responds. 'ZZ. Stop.'

She smiles at his quip.

Meanwhile, Presto Mulligan has stayed true to his profession and during his ongoing search for Rufus has performed a vanishing act.

At the other corner of the bar, recent arrival,

unorthodox ventriloquist Billy O'Brien, wearing nothing but light blue y-fronts, is engaged in a robust, and at times, heated argument with his crotch.

Ambrose walks over to Roddy after taking a phone call.

'Dinny Bruce can't make it. Major flooding on his way up, just outside Limerick. Sends his apologies.'

'Fuck. We're an act short.'

'Don't worry. Ambrose Hegarty thinks of everything.'

Ambrose picks up his brown Dunnes Stores plastic bag and removes a black leather jacket.

'Thought something like this might happen. You never know in show business. Could be a once in a lifetime opportunity.'

Ambrose ruffles his mullet and puts on a pair of oversized shades. Roddy looks apprehensive.

'Remember that John Cooper Clarke meets Pam Ayres thing I mentioned a while back. Well, I've got around to reworking it a bit. Let me introduce you to comic punk performance poet rapper Fintan D. Anger!'

Roddy looks perplexed.

'Danger, get it? D. Anger? He's unpredictable!

He's mad! He's on the far side of edgy and he has a few laughs in him as well. Coming shortly to a Poetry Slam near you!'

Ambrose suddenly starts to rap. A rhythmically jarring aural assault. Ignominious B.I.G.

'I've got a rat playing the maracas in my cavity wall. Think I'll go as Marilyn Manson to that fancy dress ball. Why pirouette in a suit of armour when you're always going to fall? Because I'm Fintan D. Anger – that's all! Because I'm Fintan D. Anger – that's all!'

Twenty past eight. Still eerily quiet. But, attempting to stay positive, there is some time to go yet before the show is due to begin. In the interim Colman Hall – 'he does them all' – has turned up. Full of nervous energy, he walks over to Roddy.

'I must say when this was suggested to me initially, I was very reluctant to perform again. But I have to admit, I am quite excited by the prospect of this evening. I've been working on a new routine. I'm particularly happy with my Katie Taylor as Lady Macbeth bit.'

He walks off mumbling 'The raven himself is hoarse. That croaks the fatal entrance of Duncan under my battlements'. Sounds 100% like Colman Hall. 0% like Katie Taylor.

Colman Hall is quite pitiful, Roddy thinks. But even *his* New York accent is probably better than mine. So Roddy has faced reality and decided not to attempt his Modh Coinníollach as-a-term-of-abuse-in-a-mobster movie routine.

A strange calm envelops him. Best described as a Death Row calm. He has everything planned. He'll come on. Introduce himself. Ask the audience how they feel tonight. Are they looking forward to a 'Truly Awful Comedy Show'? That will get an ironic cheer. Then he'll try and warm them up. Get the audience to holler and then test the level on the specially designed 'Hollerometer' contraption. This is basically a painted cardboard cube Ambrose has constructed from a Rice Krispies box. He'll praise the audience, tell them their yells come to a seven on the 'Hollerometer' and then ask them to holler just one more time. They will oblige, as he figures audiences adore this sort of interaction. He's seen it many times before at gigs. Then, he'll tell them it is a nine on the 'Hollerometer' and he will ask them to give themselves a big round of applause because they are such a great crowd. Nicely warmed up now, he'll tell them one of the things he really hates. He'll say he hates it when he looks up a builders' website and it says it is 'currently under construction'. They'll love that. His very first joke onstage. Ever. OK, it is his best joke and the one he is supposed to end his act with but better to get them laughing early. As opposed to late. Or never. Yes. They'll start to like him. Maybe, even begin to love him. And they'll love him even more when they see the other acts on the bill. That idea from Ambrose was inspired. There is no other proper comedy act on the bill for him to have to compete with. He'll be getting all the laughs tonight.

The musicians are getting bored. It is now ten-to-nine. Still, no audience member has turned up. Lead singer of The Counterfeit ZZ Top, Eoghan son of PJ, sits on the edge of the small stage.

'I work in the digitalisation department in the library of NUIG and I plastered the place with flyers. The library. The canteen. The Arts block. I thought we'd maybe get some students. I mean it's free for fuck sake.'

Ambrose, standing at the window, interjects.

'Arey, no one goes out anymore. Wedded to their devices at home. Checking their dating apps or having the auld cybersex or what have you.'

Billy O'Brien is getting cold in his underwear and has put back on his duffle coat. Placebo Domingo and his companion in the crimson fleece are sitting in the corner staring at nothing in particular. Roddy sighs. He hears footsteps. Someone is coming. An audience member. At last. A young man walks in.

'Here for the show?' Roddy asks hopefully.

'No. Sorry. Where's the upstairs Gents? There's problems with the one downstairs.'

'Oh. Just across the way. Down the corridor,' Eoghan replies.

It is nine-fifteen. All quiet on the western front. A tumbleweed convention.

Ambrose is downstairs. A much busier social environment. He is imploring the hardened regulars to break their habits of a lifetime and sample a free comedy show upstairs. No thanks, pal. One. We're not interested. Who wants to watch a bunch of fuckin' comedians or whatever ye are. Two, there's no way we'd miss the second half of that Champion's League group stage match.

Ambrose counters. But the group stages aren't that important. Anyway, we can put back the start of the show until the game ends, if you like. No dice. Then we'd miss the analysis of the match we've just seen. And then we'd miss the highlights of all the other group stage matches tonight. And then the analysis of all those matches. And then the highlights of all last night's matches! And then the analysis of last night's matches! Before watching the latest sketch from *Après Match*. Now those fellas are funny!

Ambrose returns upstairs. Shakes his head at Roddy.

'Why didn't we think of the auld soccer?' he wonders aloud.

Placebo looks over and speaks.

'If people don't want to come out, they won't come out. There is always some excuse. If there'd been no soccer tonight, it might have been raining.'

'It's just started,' Billy O'Brien announces.

'Lashing.'

'Must be that storm over Limerick Dinny Bruce got stuck in. Moving northwards,' Ambrose suggests.

'Oh. Brilliant. Won't get an audience now,' Roddy says, sighing.

'Might as well pack up,' Sully, the Counterfeit ZZ Top drummer states as he stands up.

'Where's my vest, jumper and trousers?' Billy O'Brien queries.

'What a blow-out. A disaster.' Roddy groaned. 'No more deadlines and Comedy Covenants for me. Might as well accept reality. Who am I kidding? The stand-up comedy career was all just a desperate dream.'

He stares over at Ambrose.

'And you! Don't you dare bring up that Gaudi fella!'

Roddy sits on the edge of the small stage. Hands on his head. He looks up.

'Can this evening get any worse?'

On cue, a crestfallen Presto Mulligan shuffles in slowly holding up a limp Rufus by the ears.

They all look over at him.

Presto sighs. 'They found him downstairs. In the toilet.'

There is a long silence. Then a voice is heard. In the back. In the darkness. Unmistakably, *not* Katie Taylor.

'Now take me light! Now cover my darkness! Oh woe is me! Oh fie! My life! My life!'

THE ROUNDING UP BIT AT THE END

It is five years later. The world is in flux. Agent Orange is in The White House and across the Irish Sea, Rule Britannia is fast becoming Rue Brexitannia.

Meanwhile, in an ever-laid-back Galway... Roddy sits behind the desk of Bodkin Travel, his travel agency located just down from the Christ the King Church and next to the old Claude Toft Amusement arcade in Upper Salthill. His business venture has become surprisingly successful. He set it up in 2015. As a pop-up travel agency for the older demographic. But it became so successful he decided to give it a go, full-time. There are loads of elderly people in Salthill. Getting out of their SUVs and walking around in their golf caps. Like an overcast Florida with unresolved litter problems. Agnes had given him the idea a few years ago, long before she passed away. Senior citizens are hopeless with the internet. But say if they want to go on holidays, what should they do? They should go visit Bodkin Travel. Roddy Bodkin, with extensive experience in the tourism and travel trade, will help you with all your queries and organize for you the best deal. She was some woman, Agnes. He misses his mother. Ironically, his recent share of the inheritance has ensured Bodkin Travel will remain on a secure financial footing for the near future.

Agnes started to decline about six months after that truly awful Truly Awful Comedy Club evening. It's what happens to all old people. Eventually.

One direction. (Even Niall Horan and Harry Styles will get old). No reverse gear.

Roddy noticed that things were changing gradually during his trips to Kinvara. In 2013, at the end of the visit, Agnes would drive him to the bus stop on Main Street for the bus back to Galway and he'd kiss her on the cheek goodbye. Then by early 2014, she didn't want to drive him to the bus stop anymore because she was liable to get stressed with the traffic, so she'd get up from where she was sitting in the living room, walk him to the front door and he'd kiss her on the cheek goodbye.

Then she had a couple of bad turns, late 2014. By early 2015, after a visit, she could only walk to the door of the living room, and this is where he'd kiss her on the cheek goodbye.

By mid-2015, after a visit, she couldn't walk to the door of the living room, but she could stand up from where she was sitting, which was on the sofa. At the sofa, he'd kiss her on the cheek goodbye.

By autumn 2015, it got to the stage where she couldn't stand up from the sofa. So as she remained seated on the sofa he would bend down and kiss her on the cheek goodbye.

Suddenly, the time had arrived to organize some home help. Dodged a bullet there son, Roddy would think. Or should he feel guilty about getting the hell out a few years back, before inadvertently becoming the DC? The carer's name was Jessa Mae. A compassionate hard-working lady from the Philippines. The first few months were tough, however. Agnes wanted to protect her territory and independence. Didn't want a complete stranger from an unfamiliar background looking after her. But with her diminishing powers the fight was short-lived.

Things deteriorated rapidly after that. Early 2016. Agnes could no longer go up and down the stairs so she ended up living in her bedroom. She'd spend most of the time sitting on a comfortable chair watching old TV shows on TG4 like *Rawhide* or *The Waltons*. So now, when leaving, Roddy would go into her bedroom, go over to where she was sitting, and kiss her on the cheek goodbye.

A few months later it got to the stage when Agnes couldn't even get out of her bed. She couldn't go from the bed to the chair in her bedroom. So she'd be just sitting up on the bed. Now *The Little House on The Prairie* kept her company. Roddy felt an acute wistfulness. The programmes he watched with his mother in the 1970s when he was a child and she was in the prime of her life, they were now re-watching, but under markedly different circumstances.

Then by mid-2017, Agnes couldn't even sit up on the bed. She was sinking into that bed. Roddy had to crouch down, almost on one knee to kiss her on the cheek goodbye.

Roddy was being introduced to a whole new world. A world of mental confusion. Bizarre non-sequiturs. Medical hoists. Incontinent pads. A nursing home was suggested. By Ronan. Money is not an object, he declared from Nordberg International HQ in Frankfurt. He'd been promoted and transferred there in September 2014 and was happily settled with Jenny, Ciaran and recent new addition to the family, Emma.

Roddy looked into the matter. With good

friend, forthright farmer scribbler poet Ambrose Hegarty, he spent a few days driving to various nursing homes in Ambrose's jalopy. All the nice nursing homes, the reasonably run ones (as opposed to the depressingly darkly lit under-resourced ones) in the greater Galway region were full. The only way to get a relative into one would be if a vacancy arose. 'You'll just have to kill one of the old dears,' Ambrose suggested. 'Sure, look at the state of some of them, you'd be doing them a favour.' Roddy wasn't sure if his friend was serious. Then Ambrose said something all people on the cusp of turning fifty eventually announce. I. Don't. Want. To. End. Up. Like. That. Followed swiftly by... I'd. Sooner. Kill. Myself.

Ultimately, the nursing home route wasn't needed however. A sudden bout of acute pneumonia took care of that. And now she *was* on top of Ger in Rahoon Cemetery. Roddy's bittersweet recollection of Agnes's final years is abruptly interrupted as two customers, an attractive woman and her elderly mother, enter. Roddy smiles. The customers sit down. The woman wants to organize a holiday for her mother and her mother's sister in Lanzarote.

Roddy starts his Bodkin Travel spiel and the

woman's mother listens attentively. The woman roots for a packet of cigarettes in her handbag and says she's going out for a smoke. As she gets up Roddy scrutinizes her. She stares back at him. It takes a moment but they finally recognize each other. She then berates him. Half in jest.

'I think I should march my mother out of this place, immediately. Didn't you stand me up on a Ben Stiller movie date a few years ago?'

He blushes.

'Sorry about that. Fiona, isn't it? My head was somewhere else that night.'

There is a pause. They smirk at each other as the elderly mother looks on. Finally, Roddy thinks of something to say.

'By the way, what's your favourite *Father Ted* episode?'

THE END